"Don't think we're over just because you say so."

Philip's voice was raspy. "I know you care about me as much as I care about you. How can you justify ending our relationship?"

"It's because I care that I'm doing it," she told him wearily. "To spare myself the hell I went through that day, and to spare you having a neurotic woman on your back all the time."

"I'm afraid I'm not as logical as you, Lana," he said wryly. "I can't simply order my heart to follow my head. But I don't intend to let you go that easily."

"The choice isn't yours!" She looked up at him with tear-filled eyes. "I'm making the choice, Phil—"

His name ended in a gasp as he kissed her parted lips . . . a kiss that made all words seem empty.

MADELEINE KER, one of our British authors, is a self-described "compulsive writer." In fact, Madeleine has been known to deliver six romances in less than a year. The author is married, and in addition to a writing career, is a graduate student at Durham University.

Books by Madeleine Ker

HARLEQUIN PRESENTS

HARLEQUIN ROMANCE

These books may be available at your local bookseller.

Don't miss any of our special offers. Write to us at the following address for information on our newest releases.

Harlequin Reader Service
901 Fuhrmann Blvd., P.O. Box 1397, Buffalo, NY 14240
Canadian address: P.O. Box 2800, Postal Station A,
5170 Yonge St., Willowdale, Ont. M2N 6J3

MADELEINE KER

danger zone

Harlequin Books

TORONTO • NEW YORK • LONDON
AMSTERDAM • PARIS • SYDNEY • HAMBURG
STOCKHOLM • ATHENS • TOKYO • MILAN

Harlequin Presents first edition May 1986
ISBN 0-373-10884-2

Original hardcover edition published in 1985
by Mills & Boon Limited

Printed in U.S.A.

CHAPTER ONE

LANA'S heart was in her mouth as she walked into the executive board-room of American Fashions, with her designs tucked under one silk-clad arm.

'I like people who understand that time is money,' Desiree said approvingly, ushering Lana to a chair. 'You've been very prompt.'

It was, in fact, exactly six weeks since she'd signed the contract to design a range of knitwear for the autumn season. The garments, pure and classical in line, were going to carry her own name on the labels: 'Designed by Lana Fox' on a tab of cream silk. Despite the importance of the contract to her, producing the portfolio had been a pleasure. Sweaters had always been a favourite part of her own wardrobe; they were practical, perennially modern, and the possible variations were infinite. The ideas had come thick and fast, but the big question was whether *they* were going to like the designs.

She'd already met Desiree Bruce and Michael Signa, the people who had the ultimate decision on whether or not to accept the designs for American Fashions' prestigious chain of stores. Desiree had seen Lana's designs while she was still at college last year, and had been excited enough to establish contact there and then. The three or four others present around the mahogany table were the fashion department manager and some representatives from the knitting company who were going to produce the designs.

Lana couldn't suppress the nervous fluttering of her heart as she unfolded the sketches, one after another, and explained what she had in mind.

'I wonder if these designs aren't a little too avant-garde for American Fashions,' Desiree sighed through a lungful of cigarette-smoke after ten minutes. 'Especially these tops. They're really more suitable for Paris than New York.'

'You've got a point.' Michael Signa, small and neat, held up a design for a close-fitting top with delicate openwork panels. 'Our customers tend to be more conservative than this.' He studied the garment thoughtfully as Lana waited on tenterhooks. 'But the lines are so wonderfully lithe. This is going to be beautiful in pastel pinks and greys.'

'There's an evening version of that,' Lana said hastily, seizing her opportunity with a nervous smile. She sorted quickly through the crisply rustling sheets. 'Here it is. The pattern's the same, but the colour will darken to black or navy, with metallic stripes.' Necks craned to study the design. Even in the flat colours of the sketch it was obvious that the final product would have an uncanny brilliance.

'I see,' Michael nodded, dark eyes narrowed. He glanced at Desiree.

'I've done some other versions of the same kind of thing,' Lana went on, spreading them out. Dear God, let them be impressed! She could sense their growing interest under the laconic New York manner, but she needed them to be really excited, otherwise they would never buy. 'This is a sleeveless cocktail sweater. It's really not as daring as it looks—more of a classical shape with a modern variation. So is this, just a bit longer and fuller. They could both easily be made out of silk for an even softer look.'

She spread them out, the products of her hours of work in the airy studio at her uptown apartment. Velvety black with radiating gold stripes, the cool shimmer of cream and silver, an exquisitely sheer dress in contrasting basketweave and delicate seed stitch. Her brief of simplicity hadn't stopped her from using her imagination to create a dazzling variety of moods and shapes. That was the real pleasure of designing clothes—being able to create infinite variations on a theme.

'These are nice.' Desiree Bruce peered over her glasses at the design for a pure white sweater. 'But, my God, will you look at those textures! How on earth would you make a thing like this economically?'

The woman from the knitting company shook her head with a sour expression. 'I'm afraid our machines can't handle that kind of thing, Miss Bruce. We can only do one kind of knit at a time. This is just too complicated——'

'It's not as bad as it looks.' Lana leaned forward eagerly, picking up the samples she'd knitted on her own knitting-machine. 'There are three different kinds of knit, yes, but you'll see they're all in triangles. I made these on a machine, one at a time. They just have to be sewed together by hand. Like this. Almost like a patchwork quilt. I know it'll put the price up a little, but I'm sure people will pay to have something that's unique.'

'They probably will, at that.' Michael Signa looked up at her. There wasn't just professional admiration in his eyes, but something else as well. That expression that told her he was seeing her as a woman, and a very attractive one. 'Forgive me, Lana—is this an original idea?'

'As far as I know,' she nodded. Conversation rose in a buzz all around her. Ignored all of a sudden, Lana leaned back to watch them with a huge inward sigh. After a less than promising beginning, that bright look in their eyes told her that their interest had ignited at last.

She herself had never had any doubts at all about the designs—they were ravishing! American Fashions would be able to sell every one they knitted up. They'd be marketed as exclusive designer garments for two-hundred dollars apiece; and then, at the end of the season, when The Look had been established by the chic and the rich, they'd farm the designs out for the not-so-rich, simplified and toned down, in acrylics and mixtures.

'Okay, Lana,' Desiree said at last, glancing at the manager, 'leave these with us, and we'll get back to you as soon as possible. I think I speak for all of us when I say we basically like the designs——'

'We basically *adore* the designs,' Michael said warmly. His eyes dropped to the soft swell of Lana's breasts against the sheer silk blouse she was wearing. Lana nodded her thanks impassively, trying to disguise her inner glee. She'd done it!

The meeting broke up in another buzz of conversation. Desiree Bruce was still playing it cool, but Lana could sense the excitement in the tall, angular planner. She guessed that Desiree was practically bursting to get down to the business of getting these designs on to the shelves and subsequently into those brightly-coloured boxes that American Fashions customers took home. It was the biggest and most important order she'd yet filled, and she was feeling very contented indeed with life at that moment!

'Before you go.' Mike Signa touched her arm. 'I'd like to—uh, go through a few last details, Lana. Would you care to have a cup of coffee in my office?'

'Of course,' she beamed. He rescued the designs from Desiree, and led Lana to his crowded little office with its spectacular view of the Empire State building.

'*Loved* the designs,' he said, busying himself with the percolator. 'Love all your designs. Come to think of it, love that suit you're wearing.'

'Thanks,' she said with an inner smile. Male admiration wasn't always welcome, but it could sometimes be turned to a woman's advantage. If there was anything she'd learned by having men interested in her ever since she was fifteen, that was it. Sexually, most of them were idiots!

She'd been blessed with a creamy English complexion and a face that could be startlingly beautiful at certain moments. The thick blonde hair that fell across her cheek as she bent over her designs contrasted strikingly with dark, arching eyebrows, sooty lashes, and cabochon-green eyes. Her mouth, tender as satin, was one of her best features, yet the expression on it suggested that obstinacy might be one of her faults!

Physically, she had none of the elongated, gaunt lines of the models who wore the clothes she designed for a living. There were unashamed curves at her hips and the small, high breasts that tilted so imperiously upwards, as though demanding a lover's kiss.

Under the honey-tanned skin, too, she was fit in a way which would have been considered highly unfashionable in a woman of fifty years ago. She'd always been active, adored dancing and swimming, and she carried her five-foot-two with instinctive animal grace.

'Desiree says your father's a Sir,' Michael said, a shade naïvely. 'Is he really?'

'For his sins,' Lana nodded.

'Does that make you a Lady?'

'I'm afraid not,' she replied, by now well-used to American puzzlement about the complicated British honours system. She stretched, glad to feel the tension leave her body after the conclusion of that meeting. 'It's an honour which he earned, and which will die with him.'

'That kind of thing must count for a lot in diplomatic circles?'

'I suppose it must, but probably less than you'd think. Some people naturally expect the British Consul-General to have a title and a monocle, and wear a hat with white plumes in it!'

'He doesn't?'

'Only Governor-Generals get white plumes,' she smiled. Michael Signa was obviously intrigued by her. No matter how long she lived in America—and after ten years in various parts of the States, even her accent was becoming Americanised—there was always an alien quality about her that appealed to some, irritated others.

By the time Michael had reached the point of mentioning a little Chinese restaurant he knew, she'd made up her mind that she oughtn't really to be flirting with him.

'I'm sorry, Michael,' she said aplogetically, 'but I'm all tied up tonight. I have a lot of work to finish for Nardi.'

'Sure,' he blinked, looking so downcast that Lana realised he probably imagined he'd been making a dazzling impression on her.

'Just give me a call,' she relented, partly to soothe his feelings and partly because it might be useful to have a personal contact at American Fashions. 'I do like Chinese food.'

'You're on,' he said, brightening.

Funny, she thought, how quickly men got that spaniel look in their eyes. God save her from ever looking like that at any man! 'And now,' she smiled, excusing herself, 'I really have to run, Michael. I'm meeting my father for lunch in half-an-hour.'

'I'll show you out.'

She'd always known that she was alluring to men, and yet she'd never felt much in the way of reciprocal desire. Michael, she reflected, smiling at his jokes on the way down, was not unlike John du Pont or Lionel Webber. The same kind of ambitious boy, handsome in an all-American way, and possessing enough self-confidence and push to be interesting. But that was all. She knew she'd never get excited over anyone like him—not as excited, for example, as she got over a good fashion idea! When love came, it would probably stay secondary to her career. She saw it as a nice, comfortable feeling, a nice warm feeling to come home to at the end of a working day.

Lana was a strange mixture of innocence and self-awareness. If she'd been the wanton type, she could have had as many lovers as she desired. But, thank goodness, she was a cool, calm, level-headed spinster who neither had nor desired lovers. She simply was not the wanton type, and never would be. And that was all.

She had other ambitions entirely . . .

* * *

'You're still thinking about your own fashion house?' her father sighed as the waiter re-filled their wine-glasses. 'I hoped you'd forget all that. Aren't you doing well enough as a designer?'

'I am,' she agreed, slipping the beautifully-cut jacket off her shoulders and tackling her *filet mignon*. 'So far.'

'What does that mean?' he enquired, blue eyes watching her shrewdly. Wetherby Fox was a burly man made distinguished by a mane of white hair and a beaky, aristocratic profile, and he had exceptionally piercing eyes which only softened these days when he was looking at his daughter. Since her mother's death nine years ago, he'd raised her singlehanded, and there was a strong bond between them.

'The truth is,' Lana sighed, looking at him affectionately, 'that the whole fashion world is inherently flimsy, dearest Dad. It's fickle, just like any other form of showbusiness. Today's brilliant young star suddenly becomes tomorrow's nobody.'

'Not unlike international diplomacy,' her father put in drily. The restaurant was filling rapidly, and he had to lean forward to make his gruff voice heard. 'Of course, you know the solution.'

'Find some hapless husband to look after me for the rest of my life?' she smiled.

'Exactly.'

'Not a chance! I intend to become a lady of independent means, and you know it.'

'All too well.' He was old-fashioned enough to have as his chief ambition for her that she would settle down and marry some rich young man, and turn into a respectable married matron. He'd been dropping hints ever since she'd left high school.

That she'd wanted to design clothes for a living was bad enough; the idea of starting a business on her own was much worse! 'All too well,' he repeated glumly as she leaned across to spear one of his potatoes. 'Mind telling me why the food on *my* plate is always more interesting than the food on yours?'

'We were discussing my business future,' she reminded him adroitly.

'I've spoiled you rotten,' he sighed. 'Ah well. Someday you'll see sense. But won't going into business for yourself simply compound the problems you've mentioned? For one thing, you'll be coming up against some very stiff competition.'

'If I can sell my designs to shops like American Fashions and Susanna Nardi,' Lana pointed out with faultless logic, 'I can sell them direct to the public.' She smiled at her father, eyes glinting. 'Besides, someone else takes all the profit that way. They pay me a set amount for each design, whether they sell one garment or a hundred. Why shouldn't I be able to make money on my own success?'

'You're turning out a remarkably shrewd little minx,' Wetherby Fox observed, patting his silver moustache with his napkin. 'Something's obviously sharpening your wits, though whether it's working at a job or living on your own I can't exactly say.'

He smiled at her, giving her a moment to reflect that he was looking rather tired these days. Sir Wetherby Fox had been appointed Consul-General in New York around the time of Lana's graduation, and they'd moved up from Chicago together. Her father lived at the palatial Consul's house, of course, but Lana had wanted to be independent of the ceaseless diplomatic bustle that went on around her father. She'd adapted well enough to America to want to make it on her own now. When she'd come to Manhattan to live, she'd needed a place big enough to include a studio for her to work in, and the airy, roomy apartment on the still-shabby upper West Side had been a perfect solution.

'You have to be shrewd in New York,' Lana commented. 'It's a rat-race.' She glanced around the opulent restaurant with bright green eyes. 'The only difference is that the rats wear mink coats in this town.'

'And you'd like them to wear mink coats designed by Lana Fox,' her father suggested with a wry smile.

'I'm serious about this, Dad. Deep down, I know that going independent would be the best thing for me. I'm at my happiest and most creative when I can work to my own standards and to no-one else's.' She waved slender fingers. 'I'm not talking about a fashion empire. Just a small, compact production unit, producing original, high-quality fashionwear at a reasonable price. It can't fail,' she said, enthusiasm flushing her cheeks as she relished the picture she'd conjured up. 'It'll be a runaway success, I know it!'

'All right.' He pushed his plate away, making a space on the table. 'If you're really serious about this, I'm prepared to help you investigate the idea. But you'll need a lot of professional advice, not to mention the question of financial backing. And no——' he said firmly, putting up a hand, 'I'm far too busy and too poor to give you either. You're going to have to do this on your own.'

'I wouldn't have dreamed of asking you,' Lana said innocently.

'Not much, you wouldn't.' He took a note-pad from his inside pocket, and began writing out an address. 'There's a man you ought to talk to about this, Lana. His name's Philip Casson. He's an English banker, but he has strong American connections, and he happens to be in New York right now. If you can interest him, he'll give you the best advice available. Would you like me to arrange a meeting?'

'I'll ring him myself,' Lana said, taking the slip of paper eagerly. 'Philip Casson. Is he really good?'

'In this particular field, he's one of the best,' her father assured her. 'He runs the London Corporate Bank. It's not one of the giant merchant banks, but they're ultra-efficient. When I had that inheritance from your great-uncle a few years ago, I was advised to go to Casson, and he's done wonders with the investment ever since. If anyone can help you, he can.' He watched her eager face with a paternal smile. 'But that depends, of course, on your convincing him of your worthiness—and he's a tough customer!'

'Leave that to me,' she said meaningfully, folding the address away.

'I intend to. Let me know what he suggests, will you?'

'I sure will,' Lana promised, already planning how she would tackle the tough Mr Casson.

'I *certainly* will,' her father corrected with a pained expression. 'Try and talk English—the Queen's variety. And now,' he went on, reaching for the menu, 'I realise that you eat, drink and sleep fashion, but shall we turn our attention to the demanding subject of pudding?'

She said goodbye to her father an hour later

and made her way back towards her apartment, the banker's address safely in her bag, the first step in making her dream a reality. She'd expected her father to know the best man to approach. New York was a place where anything, and everything, could come true.

So far she'd adored the city. She'd felt an immediate sympathy with the place, possibly because its history had more meaning for her than most American cities. A branch of the Fox family had emigrated to New York in the eighteenth century. Their tombstones still stood in the venerable cemetery at Trinity Church, a green oasis in the downtown bustle of Wall Street. Her father had taken her to see the weathered gravestones when they'd first come to New York.

New York had something no other place in the world had, a living excitement that went on day and night. Besides, it was the very hub of the American fashion scene, and anyone who was anyone simply *had* to live in New York, where the biggest fashion shows took place, where money and society were so perfectly poised. And even if the Big Apple occasionally turned out to be more like an overripe tomato, it was still one of the great cultural centres of the world.

She got home, plucked up her courage, and dialled Philip Casson's number at once. The secretary who answered was hesitant about putting her through, but at last a deep, unmistakably authoritative voice came on to the line.

'Philip Casson.'

'Oh—good afternoon, Mr Casson,' Lana said, nervously, far from sure of herself. 'My name's Lana Fox. You don't know me—I'm Wetherby Fox's daughter.'

'The British Consul-General?'

'That's right.' Her palm was clammy around the receiver. 'I hope you don't mind my ringing you. My father gave me your name this morning, and suggested I consult you about—about an idea I have.'

'What sort of idea?'

'I—I'm a fashion designer,' she told him, twisting the cord restlessly round her finger, and trying not to sound clumsy. 'I design clothes for fashion houses and shops, people like that. I've been doing quite well—very well, I mean—and now I want to start up a business of my own, manufacturing my own clothes.'

'I see. Very commendable.' The accent was English, yet it held a smoky American undertone, not unlike her own. 'How can I help you?'

'Dad—my father thought you might be able to advise me on—on the practical side of things.'

'You're talking about finance?'

She drew a breath. 'Yes, Mr Casson. I'm talking about finance and general advice. I wonder if I could make an appointment to see you some time?'

'Well——' He sounded dubious. 'I don't usually do this sort of work in New York. I do finance projects like the one you're proposing, but mainly in England. My business in New York is mainly investment counselling. Where were you thinking of setting up this business?'

'Here, in New York,' she said unhappily.

'I don't have a full-scale branch in Manhattan, Miss Fox. One's being set up, but it won't be ready for some time yet. That means I have a limited amount of staff at my disposal here.' The deep voice was friendly but not even slightly interested. 'It would really be better if you went to your own bank manager in New York.'

'I understand that,' she said urgently, feeling that she was on the brink of being shrugged off. 'But my father seems to have a lot of confidence in you, Mr Casson. I really would be *most* grateful if you could spare me an hour or so.'

He laughed shortly. 'We might be wasting each other's time.'

'Oh no—not *my* time, anyway,' she said, struggling not to lose his interest. 'I'd appreciate your advice very much indeed.'

He grunted. 'I'll check my diary.' There was a pause, and Lana waited on tenterhooks. 'Most of my time's taken up over the next week or two, Miss Fox,' he went on slowly. 'There are a lot of projects claiming my attention just lately.'

'Oh.' Her hopes wilted.

'However, I generally take a swim at the Hilton around lunch-time. Perhaps we can meet there for a drink some time this week?'

'At the Hilton?' she blinked.

'The rooftop pool. There's a restaurant and a bar at the poolside. If you don't mind the informal setting, that is——'

'Not at all!' she beamed.

'Good. When would suit you?'

'Tomorrow,' Lana suggested promptly, striking while the iron was at least lukewarm.

'Tomorrow it is, then,' he said with the ghost of a laugh. 'About one-fifteen. Ask one of the waiters to show you to my usual table.'

'Thank you,' Lana said gratefully, her green eyes bright. 'I really appreciate that, Mr Casson——'

'I look forward to seeing you then.' The line

clicked dead in her ear, and she jumped up
excitedly. It was turning out her day—and what
better place to start the future than the New York
Hilton!

She danced through to her studio, dreaming of
the clothes she would make. Racks and racks of
them, dazzling and exciting, coloured like the
rainbow, swishing and rustling with the eager
hands of customers sorting through them. And her
meagre bank-balance, swelling comfortably as the
dollars rolled in. Fame and fortune. *Vogue*.
Harper's.

She plumped herself down in front of her
drawing board, and soon her pencil was racing
eagerly across the paper in time with her thoughts.
Since graduating from design college in Chicago a
year or so previously, her career had been growing
with the vigour of a bean-plant.

Of course, she'd started right out at the
beginning with an unfair advantage over every
other student in her fashion class. She'd grown up
in a world of considerable richness. Being a
diplomat's daughter had enabled her to mix with
the cultured and the privileged all over the world.
Her mother had had the taste to stay at the
forefront of the fashionable world until her early
death from cancer. Her father had a well-
developed and eclectic taste for music, art, good
food and good company. It was only natural that
their only daughter should reach maturity with a
highly-developed sense of style. A blazing talent
for designing striking clothes had made her choice
of career obvious.

Her own design workshop was the logical next
stage. She was outgrowing her present career with
startling rapidity. She didn't need to work to

anyone else's dictates any more, not when she had a better idea of the important fashion trends than many buyers. She wanted to make her own decisions from now on.

And she knew they'd be the right ones.

CHAPTER TWO

SHE was determined to succeed as she set off the next day around eleven-thirty to meet Philip Casson. She'd dressed in immaculate summer white, and had made herself up with the detailed care of an actress rehearsing for an audition—which was what it amounted to. She was going to knock his eye out, she promised herself, blowing a kiss to her own image in the Porsche's rear-view mirror.

The Hilton car-park was jammed full with Cadillacs and Rolls Royces, so she had to leave the ice-blue car on a yellow line on York Street.

She walked back to the magnificent hotel, and took the lift right up to the roof, her heart thudding. It *had* to go right for her!

Emerging from the lounge, Lana took off her sunglasses, and stared across the roof-top pool area. The day was hot and brilliantly sunny, and the heat rose off the paved poolside in a wave, making the sparkling blue water all the more appealing.

It was busy, but not with the sort of people who constituted anything so vulgar as a crowd. Gold sparkled against tanned skin, Paris hats shaded expensive face-lifts from the sun. If she could open a boutique up here, Lana thought wryly, she'd be made!

This was bound to be a congregating-place for the Beautiful People. If you had the figure for it, you reclined in a deck-chair in the skimpiest of costumes, showing off your tan. If you didn't, you sheltered at one of the umbrella-shaded tables and kept cool with a long drink and the thought of what all this was costing you per day.

A waiter materialised at her side.

'Table for one, ma'am?'

'I'm meeting someone,' she told him. 'A Mr Philip Casson.'

The name was obviously familiar. 'Right this way, ma'am.'

Lana followed his white-coated figure through the potted yuccas and ornamental palms to a table at the far side of the pool. The skyscraperscape of New York made an unlikely panorama for the Palm Beach atmosphere, but there weren't *too* many buildings taller than the Hilton to overlook it.

The table was vacant except for a towelling-robe neatly laid out on one chair. No Mr Casson. 'Is he here yet?' she asked the waiter anxiously.

'Mr Casson's right over there.' She followed the pointing finger, and found herself looking at a man's bronzed and muscular back some twenty feet away.

He was sitting at the bar, talking to a blonde who was doing a fair imitation of the Coppertone ad. 'Shall I call him over?'

'No,' she said quickly, wanting time to observe him. 'I'll just wait.'

'Can I get you a drink, ma'am?'

'Just fruit-juice, please.'

'Right away.' The waiter bowed, leaving her.

She sat back, assessing Philip Casson through narrowed eyes while she waited for him to notice her. What would be the best strategy? A man like that would probably respond to flirtation. He'd probably expect flirtation, in fact—he looked as though he had an oversized ego! She might even have been better off with a hip-hugging, cleavage-revealing dress than her sober suit.

He was tanned and tough-looking, and at least ten years older than she was. Early thirties? At that moment he was laughing at something the woman was saying, and the laughter-lines had softened what she instinctively guessed would be a cruel face in repose.

The eyebrows curved in lines that spoke of a dangerous temper, the eyelashes were thick and black, the face lean and—Lana hesitated. Strong. That was it. The face of a man of the world, the well-defined etching of lines suggesting that he'd had plenty of experience. In all departments, and not all of it easy. The hair, very dark and shot with grey, confirmed that, but his shoulders and back were muscled, carved mahogany; he had the body of an athlete.

Just then he looked up. The eyes that met hers were a deep, tawny green. Their directness was animal, startling. Lana tensed automatically, then raised a hand in greeting. He waved briefly to her, excused himself from the blonde, and came over towards her. Right, she told herself with a flutter of nerves, summon up all your charm, girl!

He was taller than she'd expected, the black costume emphasizing, rather than concealing his manhood. The tangle of dark hair on his chest was slightly shocking.

'Miss Fox?'

'That's right,' she said, rising. His grip was strong and cool, as though he were judging her in some way by her handshake right from the start. 'Thank you for seeing me,' she told him. 'I know just how busy you must be, and I'm sorry if I've interrupted anything——'

He waved her apologies away. 'I was simply talking to a friend,' he said in the charming, deep voice she remembered from their earlier conversation. 'I've already had my swim. Very beneficial. After a morning in the Stock Exchange I really need to stretch my body a little.'

'I'm sure you do.' Lana glanced at his lean, formidably male near-nakedness. He had something she'd only seen in very successful people—a presence. It would have made him remarkable even if he'd been short and plain, and not devastatingly male. 'This is a very glamorous place to do your stretching in,' she commented brightly.

'It's not my idea of a place to exercise.' He shrugged, pulling on the robe and indicating her to sit. 'But it impresses the hell out of my clients.' His wicked smile made him suddenly handsome as Lucifer, those vivid green eyes glinting as though they knew every secret of her soul. 'Have you ordered a drink?'

'Yes, thank you,' she smiled, wondering just how you got around to flirting with a man like Philip Casson. He must be so used to women gawking at him; and she was hardly the most expert *femme fatale* in New York.

So this beautiful animal was the man whose judgment her father trusted so implicitly! 'You're not exactly what a merchant banker is expected to look like——' she began, then stopped in embarrassment, realising she'd been thinking aloud.

He took a slim gold watch from his pocket and clipped it around his wrist. His hands were excellent, strong yet precise. 'You're not exactly what a hard-nosed businesswoman is supposed to look like, either,' he commented, looking up at her with a half-smile on his full, strong mouth. 'You're about ten years younger than I expected.'

'How old did you expect me to be?' Lana asked, slightly put out.

'In your thirties. Which makes you just over twenty.' The way he put it made it a subtle question.

'I'm twenty-two,' she confirmed, meeting his eyes squarely. 'But I'm not too young to be thinking of starting a business, Mr Casson, I promise you!'

'Of course you aren't. I have a seventeen year-old client who's already made a million out of three pop singles,' he smiled, the pupils dark in his green eyes. 'So, you're a fashion designer,' he went on. 'Chicago College of Design, *summa cum laude*. You've been out of college barely a year, but you've already made a name for yourself. Designs for Susanna Nardi on Fifth Avenue, the Carlton Collection, a daring exhibition at the World Trade Centre. And coming up soon, the Autumn Show, one of the top fashion events of the year.' He ignored her startled expression. 'You certainly have ambition, and you seem to know what you want out of life. You've even bought yourself a Porsche this year—second-hand, but still quite classy for a twenty-two year-old.'

'You've been checking up on me!' Lana

protested breathlessly, somewhat shocked at the calm précis of her life and character.

'Of course,' he replied, lowering ridiculously long eyelashes as though embarrassed at her naïveté. 'As soon as you called me I had my secretary run a brief check on you.' The waiter arrived with Lana's drink. Without having to be asked, she noticed, he'd also brought a vodka and tonic for her host.

Philip Casson signed the bill, then raised his glass to her. 'Health.'

'Cheers.' Lana drank, feeling rather uncomfortably that Mr Casson of the London Corporate Bank had given himself a distinct advantage already. It was disconcerting to find that he'd already formed an opinion of her—but also exciting to realise that he'd at least taken her seriously enough to check her out. 'I didn't think you were that interested,' she confessed innocently.

'With a record like that,' he shrugged, 'you'd have come to me with good recommendations even if you hadn't been Wetherby Fox's daughter.'

Lana smiled weakly. 'You mean you'd have decided to lend me money on the strength of my father's name alone?'

'I haven't decided to lend you a penny yet,' he corrected her in a velvety voice, putting his glass down. 'It was merely a statement of interest. There's a long way to go before either of us make any decisions.'

'Oh,' she said, chastened. The Hilton roof-top was an unusual place to be discussing this kind of hard business, but then, Philip Casson was obviously an unusual man. There was a sense of purpose, almost of danger, in him. It showed in his face; all the features were strong, the cheekbones almost as exotic as an Apache's. The sensuality of the carved lips was emphasized by eyes that only had to close slightly to become terrifyingly fierce. A face expressing a formidable male character, and one which any woman would look at twice. Yet she felt instinctively that he used it to mask his real emotions.

'First of all,' he said, opening a small note-pad, 'I need to know what size you plan this undertaking to be. Are you thinking in terms of a small factory?'

'Oh no. More like a workshop,' Lana told him. 'I'd need at least two industrial-type sewing machines, and at least two knitting machines capable of doing intarsia and lace. Preferably computer-controlled ones that could do graphic designs. That would mean a staff of two to four machinists. In addition, I'd need two dressmakers, and maybe someone to help with the cleaning and general to-ing and fro-ing.' She drew a deep breath. 'I reckon I can deal with the marketing side myself.' She thought back on the amount of leg-work she'd done over the past twelve months. 'I've been flogging my designs for a year, and it won't be much different flogging ready-made models.'

He was making notes with a gold pen now, eyes thoughtful.

'That's clear enough. What sort of premises?'

'At least two cutting-rooms, of course, and an office if possible, nothing more.'

'And what sort of salaries would you expect to pay your staff?'

She gave him an estimate, based on around one and a half times the factory rate. She was going to need top-quality staff if this was to have any hope

of succeeding. Now that they were getting to the
actual costs, which she already knew were going to
be high, her nerves were tightening. It was a lot of
money.

'Can you give me some idea as to the sort of
production-scale you've got in mind, and what
sort of profits you'd be likely to make?'

He asked several more questions, each one
biting to the heart of the matter. She'd thought
about this long enough to have most of the
answers at her fingertips, but she was beginning to
wish she'd prepared for this interview a lot more
carefully in other ways—such as in presenting
herself as a sophisticated adult, rather than an
impulsive kid. Finally, he capped the pen and
leaned back.

'I'll check this through over the next day or so,
and work out some figures. I suggest you do the
same. You realise that I can't give you a direct
answer here and now?'

'Yes,' she nodded, biting her lip.

'But the basic idea seems to be interesting. We
can compare notes in a few days' time, and
perhaps agree on some definite proposals. Okay?'

'Okay,' she nodded, feeling a twinge of
excitement nibble at her nerves. At least he hadn't
brushed her off; and she knew instinctively that he
wasn't the sort of man who would give her empty
promises—this was a man with a sense of real
purpose about him.

'Which brings us to the administrative side of
things. I don't suppose you have much experience
of accounting?' he enquired.

'Well—I'm not completely inexperienced. I've
had to run my own affairs since I started working.
I admit it's been relatively simple so far. But I

don't see any problems handling the finances of a small business like the one I'm planning.'

'Don't you?' He tapped the pen on the table, green eyes speculative. 'One thing came out in my check on you, Miss Fox. You have expensive tastes.'

'Do I?' She blinked guiltily.

'Silk suits and a Porsche in your first year? That doesn't argue a great deal of money-sense.'

'Gold watches and lunchtime swims at the Hilton aren't exactly frugal,' she retorted pointedly, nettled by the implication.

'I don't have to be frugal,' he said calmly. 'I'm extremely wealthy, and I get a great deal of pleasure out of indulging my whims. You, on the other hand, are barely starting out on the long and winding road of life.'

'A minute ago you said I was a good proposition,' she protested, feeling she had a right to be hurt. 'Now you're saying I'm a spendthrift!'

'Porsches are durable cars,' he said obliquely. 'I'm simply advising you not to move on to a Ferrari as soon as you sell your first order. We have to understand certain things right from the start. People launching themselves out in business have to keep a very tight rein on their finances, and brilliant young designers are no exception.'

'I understand that,' Lana said, feeling sullen.

'What I'm getting at,' he smiled, 'is that you're not asking me to invest money in a factory so much as in *you*. Your talent, your personality, if you like. Before I invest large sums of money in Lana Fox, I need to know, for both your sake and the Bank's, that the investment is going to be safe.'

'Oh,' she said quietly.

'As I see it, you'll be needing capital amounting

to several thousand dollars,' he went on, sliding his hands into his pockets. 'Not to mention a great deal of my time and my staff's time. What sort of collateral can you offer?'

'You mean security?' she asked, unpleasantly taken aback by the question. Until a minute ago, she'd really thought she had this interview in the bag!

'Yes. Apart from your genius—and the Porsche, which you're buying on credit, and which therefore doesn't count.' Looking as though he was enjoying himself, he smiled lazily. 'Your apartment is rented, of course. I take it you've saved something up to show you're serious about this?'

Lana thought of the three-thousand hard-earned dollars in her current account. She'd anticipated that question with some gloom.

'Well actually,' she said unhappily, 'I don't have a great deal.' She shot him a quick look. 'But since you've been studying my affairs so carefully, you probably know that, Mr Casson.'

'I know you have just over three-thousand in your account,' he nodded, unabashed. 'Are you prepared to sink that into this project?'

'You mean the lot?' she asked in a small voice. He nodded calmly. Her heart sank right down into her neat court shoes. It would be very hard. But she had to show him she was serious about this, otherwise she'd lose him here and now. 'Of course,' she said, trying to look as though the words hadn't hurt. 'If you really think it's necessary——'

'I do.' He looked into her eyes coolly. 'Could I have a cheque?'

'A—cheque?'

'For the three-thousand,' he said, looking surprised. 'I'm about to do a feasibility study on your proposal, Miss Fox. That research will cost money—your three-thousand will just start paying the bills. I think it's the least you can do, don't you?'

Feeling dazed, Lana took the cheque-book out of her handbag. God help her! She was getting into deeper waters than she'd ever anticipated! 'Who—who shall I make it out to?' she stammered.

'The London Corporate Bank.'

She wrote the cheque out, realising with a wave of depression that she'd only have a couple of hundred dollars left in her account now. This man had better be worth the trust she was putting in him!

She stared at the cheque for a moment, fighting down her doubts, and then tore it out and handed it to him.

'There,' she said glumly.

'Thank you.' He took the cheque from her, examined it—and then calmly tore it into pieces.

'What are you *doing*?' she gasped in horror.

'I'm sorry,' he said gently, 'that must have been like pulling a tooth out. I don't need your three-thousand dollars, Miss Fox. But I did need to know how determined you are about this.' His curved, sensual mouth wore a smile with ease as he dropped the pieces into the ash-tray. 'Try and forgive my devious ways. They save a lot of time.'

'Devious!' She sat back, not knowing whether to laugh or be furious. Devious was a polite way of putting it! 'That was a genuinely horrible moment, Mr Casson,' she sighed. 'And I don't think I'm going to forgive you just yet.'

'But at least we both know how committed you are,' he pointed out mildly. In this wealthy poolside world, she thought suddenly, he was like a panther among fluffy Persian cats. He challenged her appraisal. 'You're staring, Miss Fox. Have I really offended you?'

'Not really,' she said warily, 'but you're very direct.'

'That's why I'm rich and powerful,' he nodded. His arrogance, she knew, was only partly self-mockery. Underneath it, Philip Casson was as hard as nails. 'Your father has had investments with my Bank for some time,' he went on. 'That's easily good enough for me. As a matter of fact, your father and I have met in England several times. But I didn't know he had a daughter until you called me.' He studied her, again giving her the feeling that he was appraising her carefully. 'I hardly expected you to be so beautiful.'

'Oh.' The blunt statement coming straight out of the businesslike discussion made her blink, then flush slightly. 'Thank you,' she nodded coolly.

Philip smiled. 'You look as though no one's ever said that to you before.'

'One or two have done,' she said drily, a great deal more cautious with him now than she'd been when she'd first sat down at this table!

'I'll bet they have. Are you free any night this week?'

'Free?' Lana studied his face. 'I suppose so—why?'

'I thought we'd go out for a drink somewhere,' he said calmly.

'To discuss this project?' she asked, an edge to her voice. Was this another unexpected test of her character?

'Not at all. To get better acquainted.'

'If your invitation doesn't have anything to do with the business at hand,' she suggested coolly, 'then I don't think it's very proper.'

'Oh?' He cocked his head. 'Why isn't it proper?'

'That ought to be obvious,' she said evenly, still suspicious. 'A bank manager who issues an invitation to an unattached woman who's asking him for a loan might be accused of putting unfair pressure on her.'

Philip laughed softly. 'There's no "might" about it, Lana. I *am* putting unfair pressure on you. But I'm very glad to hear that you're unattached.'

His sense of humour didn't appeal to her in the slightest, and she almost said so. 'I'm afraid I can't go anywhere with you, Mr Casson——' she began.

'We're two Britons in New York,' he interrupted gently. 'Don't you trust me? I may not be the most moral man in the world, but I don't go around seducing my clients—or British Consul-Generals' daughters.' She dropped her eyes. 'Besides, if you refuse to come out with me, I'll throw your application out of the window!'

'I see.' She bit her lip, not certain how serious he was behind that Cheshire-cat smile. If he was teasing her, then she was overreacting stupidly. Yet she knew she had a right to be annoyed at his presumption. Either way, the best way to handle this was to stay cool.

'Very well,' she said slightly stiffly, making up her mind that it was definitely worth keeping on the right side of him. After- all, he hadn't made up his mind yet, and there was a long way to go. If she could confirm his lady-killing self-image, she might have a better chance of succeeding. 'If you insist.'

'Oh, I do insist,' he said with a glint of amusement. 'Choose your night.'

'Oh——' She shrugged. 'Wednesday.'

'Excellent.' He rose, giving her the clearest possible indication that the meeting was terminated. 'I look forward to Wednesday, then.' He tapped the notes he'd made. 'And I have to say I'm more enthusiastic about your project than I anticipated. I'll draw up some figures, Lana, and ask my staff to make the appropriate enquiries in the meantime. It won't take long, I promise. Please give my regards to your father.'

'I will do.' Lana stood up, wobbly after the tension of the past half-hour. She was just beginning to realise how expertly she'd been handled. Her initial impression of a charming, easy-going man had been modified into wary respect of a highly complex and powerful personality. Next to her father, he had the most disconcerting eyes she'd ever seen, and she was certain he could see right through to her reaction to him—and was laughing quietly at her. 'Goodbye, Mr Casson.'

'Philip, please,' he corrected her. 'We're practically old friends.'

Well, she thought drily as he escorted her to the lift, Philip Casson was certainly the most interesting man she'd met in a long, long while! 'Then goodbye, Philip,' she said, offering him her hand again. 'Thank you for seeing me.'

'It was a pleasure. You're something of a rarity in New York, you know. An English virgin, cool as spring-water.'

She stepped into the lift-car, holding her bag in front of her with both hands, and nodded. The brushed-steel doors closed, leaving her with the memory of a faintly mocking smile.

An English virgin, cool as spring water. Lana glanced up the towering hotel she'd just left, both irritated and amused by that edged description. Apart from one or two sticky moments, the interview had gone well enough to make her want to dance and sing in the street. It couldn't have gone much better for her, in fact. She had a gut-feeling that Philip Casson had liked her, or had at least been intrigued by her. She had every right to her feeling of triumph. But was her virginity really that damned obvious?

In Chicago, even at her boarding-school in Devon, she'd had plenty of boyfriends. True, she'd never experienced more than a passing interest in any of them, but her reactions had been completely normal. Every girl, she presumed, enjoyed kissing and cuddling. Some girls simply didn't go all the way, though, and she was one of them. A virgin, yes; but if Philip thought she was some kind of wide-eyed innocent, he had another think coming. She could handle any Don Juan with ease!

Two or three years ago, she'd have classed Philip Casson as an 'adult', herself as 'a kid'. Now she was in the adult class herself dealing with other adults, and doing it well.

Well, to be strictly accurate, she hadn't so much dealt with Philip as had been bulldozed by him. Still, being bulldozed by a man with as much force of personality as Philip Casson had its entertaining side, after all!

Since her mother's death, her father had allowed Lana to have most things her way. Her own beauty and talent had made her all the more self-assured. Yet it was almost refreshing to meet someone who could be quite so cool towards her!

Philip Casson was the stuff dreams were made of; and while she wasn't the dreamy type, it made her heart race just a little to think he might be interested in her. Anyway, there couldn't be any harm in enjoying his undeniably thrilling company if they were to be business partners, more or less. She was in awe of him, yes; but for the first time ever she'd met a man who didn't fall flat at her feet from the word go, and that offered a distinct escape from boredom!

As she expected, the stimulation of her meeting with Philip Casson expressed itself in an explosion of lively ideas when she got back to her studio. As she wrestled to get the designs right on her sewing-machine, she was deep in her favourite fantasy again—those eager customers, clamouring for her designs. Except that the fantasy was growing more like a reality with each day that passed!

She drove across town to report back to her father that evening, squatting on the leather armchair in his study to tell him the good news before dinner.

Sir Wetherby Fox looked at his daughter speculatively as she concluded. 'Very promising indeed, Lana. Sounds like you're in, if you ask me. You must have done a good job of convincing Philip. What did you make of him, by the way?'

'He's very impressive,' Lana admitted, looking up from under her fringe of blonde hair. 'Very impressive. But a tough customer, I think.'

'You think right,' he nodded with a smile. 'If anyone can keep you in line, Philip will. You liked him?'

'I don't know if you *can* like a man like Philip

Casson,' Lana sighed. She extended one booted leg, studying the elegant toe absently. 'He's a little too awesome. I got the impression that he's something of a Don Juan.'

'Oh?'

She looked up. 'He insisted on taking me out this week.'

Her father chuckled. 'That doesn't make him a Don Juan—just a courteous host.'

She looked unconvinced. 'It makes him a fast worker, at any rate.'

'Now that's a positive advantage,' he smiled. 'I've got a lot of admiration for Philip.'

'As a man?' she probed, interested in her father's opinion.

'As a man, and as a banker. His father was a senior Army man, you know. A member of my club in London. Philip's got a lot of old Peter Casson in him.'

'Does Philip go to your stuffy old club?' Lana asked curiously, trying to picture Philip's vibrancy among the leather armchairs and ancient oil-paintings.

'Perhaps he doesn't find it quite as stuffy as you do,' the Consul smiled. 'Yes, he pops in now and then. He's a valued member of the Committee—a very astute man to have around where money's concerned.'

I'll bet he is, Lana thought. 'He's very young to be a merchant banker,' she said aloud. 'Don't you have to be enormously rich in that kind of business?'

'I understand he has a helicopter and a private jet, not to mention two yachts, one of them ocean-going.'

'Oh,' Lana said.

'And his hobby is saloon-car racing—he runs his own modified Jaguar.'

'I don't call *that* very astute,' she commented acidly. 'Risking his neck in a racing-car!'

'Well,' he smiled, 'it indicates a fair level of personal wealth. Philip's what they call financially sound in the banking business. London Corporate have assets totalling several millions, otherwise your cautious old father wouldn't have dreamed of investing with them.'

'I see.' It was hard not to be awed. She was reconsidering the handsome, masculine figure she'd met at the poolside. There was power behind that façade, a lot of power.

'But where did all that money come from?' she demanded later, over dinner. 'He can't possibly have *made* it all!'

'Why not?' Her father leaned back, buttering a roll. 'You're probably a bit too young to remember the story, but it was big news at the time. Philip took over the Bank when it was at a low ebb, some years ago. It was on the verge of folding, but he quadrupled the business within a year, and had sent it soaring within two. He brought an ailing institution back to health in the most brilliant way. A genuine British success story, which has made him the darling of the financial press ever since. There's also a branch in Switzerland, and he's going to be opening a branch in New York next year. He's moving out into a very exciting new area—encouraging foreign investors to put money in British industry.'

'Very patriotic of him,' Lana said with a slight smile. 'Is that why you like him so much?'

'Partly. Philip Casson's one of a disappearing breed, a true-blue English gentleman. Hard but fair.' The expression on his face made Lana wonder suddenly whether her father hadn't ever wanted a son. 'He's what I'd call a dominant male. A natural leader with a brilliant knack of getting things to turn out his own way.'

'Ruthless, would you say?' Lana probed.

'That's a harsh word,' her father said thoughtfully. 'I think he has a powerful sense of duty. But like a lot of self-sufficient men, he doesn't seem to give a damn about what people think of him. He works hard and plays hard. Women seem to go mad about him.'

'Not this one,' Lana retorted sharply.

'No?' her father smiled.

'He's way too old for me, anyway,' Lana said dismissively.

'Yes, I suppose he is,' the Consul nodded. For some reason, his ready agreement to her own statement irritated her slightly, but she shrugged the feeling off.

'I brought some designs to show you,' she said, rummaging through the bag she'd brought from her apartment. 'Look at these coats I dreamed up. Won't they be fabulous?'

'They look very elegant,' he nodded, sorting through the drawings she'd spread on the table. 'Beautiful, in fact. You've got such a talent.'

'Oh Dad,' she said with a sigh, 'I can't wait to be producing my own clothes!'

'You ought to be producing grandchildren for me,' he grumbled, sorting through the designs.

'What, before I get married?' she enquired with a gamine grin.

'No,' he growled, 'after you get married. Is Lionel Webber still your beau?'

'Well,' she smiled, 'I play tennis with Lionel

fairly regularly. But I wouldn't call him my beau, Dad.'

'More's the pity,' came the reply. 'He's a nice young man.'

'You mean a rich young man.' The Webber fortune, based in a series of Dallas oilfields, was vast, and Lionel Webber Junior was what her mother would have called a deb's delight. He also, though she refrained from saying this to her father, spent most of his time trying to be overly macho, which sometimes got on her nerves. She'd always been surrounded by men, and macho performances didn't impress her in the slightest.

'Anyway, I'm having a great time without being tied down,' she went on. 'There are all sorts of people besides Lionel, and I see a lot of May Baragli.'

'Good.' They got up to let the butler clear the table. 'By the way, Lana, are you going to be free in the middle of next month?'

'I can make myself free,' she nodded.

'Why not come and spend the weekend, then? I'm throwing a little cocktail party on Saturday the twenty-third, and I want you to be there.'

'Oh.' That was a slight disappointment. The Consul's usual notion of a 'little cocktail party' was something extending to fifty guests and a banquet. She'd much rather have the peace of a weekend with her father in the beautiful house, relaxing in the garden or at the poolside. 'That'll be nice.'

'It will be,' he promised, laughing. 'It'll be small and intimate, Lana. I guarantee. Not one of the big affairs you detest so much.'

'Sure,' she said wryly. 'Do I have to play hostess?'

'Susan will take care of all that,' he assured her. 'I just want you to be there and have fun.'

'That doesn't sound too taxing,' she smiled. Susan Bates was the Consul's personal secretary, an efficient brunette in her late twenties who performed some of the official functions that Lana's mother would once have performed. 'Who's coming?'

'A lot of eligible bachelors,' he replied calmly. 'At least one bank, an oil-well, and a few dozen corporations.'

'Oh, Daddy!'

He chuckled. 'Don't "Oh, Daddy" me. Just turn up.'

CHAPTER THREE

THE nightclub was smoky, the haunting wail of a saxophone rising over the buzz of conversation and laughter. The little alcove they were snugged into was obviously the best place in the house; if there was a single quality that made Philip Casson outstanding, Lana reflected, it was style. From the minute he'd picked her up at her apartment, she'd been swept off her feet by his charm, the easy way he made everything turn out smoothly. She'd been taken out by dozens of men, but none of them had been remotely like this one. The romance of the evening had quite bewitched her.

She laughed a little breathlessly. 'You certainly know how to do things *à la mode*,' she said. 'I'm not exactly used to champagne and caviare.'

Philip smiled, refilling her glass. 'What a pity it would be to get used to champagne and caviare,' he said. 'It would just become a cliché. But on special occasions——' He took a spoonful of the delicious, formidably expensive stuff from the silver bowl that rested on its bed of crushed ice between them, and spread it on to a piece of Melba toast. 'Forget the cost and eat up,' he commanded, passing it to her.

She closed her eyes, chewing the exquisite morsel, the husky note of the saxophone washing over her. The champagne she'd already drunk was going to her head.

'You're spoiling me,' she reproached him half-heartedly.

'Not at all. This comes under the heading of entertaining a client.'

Well, if this was the primrose path to hell, it was certainly a wonderful way to go! 'Is this how you always live?' she asked dreamily.

'You mean nightclubs and champagne?' He shook his head. 'It's fun now and then. But I couldn't do this all the time. Only when I want to seduce a particularly delectable virgin.' Lana widened her eyes in alarm, and Philip raised an ironic eyebrow. 'I'm only teasing you,' he said gently. In evening dress, he was as potently attractive as Lucifer, and she couldn't help feeling her awe of him become a powerful pull on her emotions. 'I'm glad you're enjoying yourself,' he said with a smile. 'You seemed quite indignant when I asked you out yesterday.'

'I was just surprised,' Lana said with dignity, accepting another piece of caviare-laden toast from his fingers. 'You can't blame me for being suspicious of your intentions. But I have to admit it makes a very nice change from starving in my garret.'

'You wouldn't know a garret if one bit you on the leg,' he commented drily. 'You know, I'm always interested by people who work when they don't have to. Your father gets an excellent salary. He also moves in New York's best social circles. You could be stuffing yourself with caviare practically every night, enjoying the society whirl and waiting for some millionaire to marry you. A glamorous existence, if you wanted it. Why bother with the rat-race?'

'I'm not waiting for anyone, millionaire or otherwise,' she said emphatically. 'I've got my own life to lead, Philip—and sponging off my Dad doesn't appeal to me. Besides,' she added with that sudden quick smile, 'I'm very talented, you know. The world has yet to hear from Lana Fox.'

'Indeed,' he commented, looking as though he might be amused by her cheek. 'I'd have thought you'd be lining up all the most eligible bachelors in town.'

'Hardly,' Lana scoffed, picking up her glass and watching the champagne-bubbles. She looked at him from the corner of her eye. 'The only function men have in my life is to pay for the clothes I design for their wives.'

'Well, well.' Philip's green eyes glinted. 'Brave talk.'

'Honest talk,' she retorted, looking him in the face. It was a very strong face, the face of a man who was singleminded about getting what he wanted out of life. The mouth was both cruel and passionate, the stare of those wolf's eyes disconcertingly direct. Piercing. Under the silk jacket, she knew, his body was tanned, iron-hard——

'What are you looking at?' he challenged.

'I was just wondering what the girls at my boarding-school would have made of you,' she said unguardedly. 'They thought anyone was gorgeous who had wealth, or power, or a handsome face, or sex-appeal. I suppose that makes you ultra-gorgeous.' She looked away from him, flushing as she realised that the heady wine had loosened her tongue treacherously!

'Not that any of these things affect you,' he said with veiled mockery.

'That's right,' she said defiantly, pretending to be looking at the band, and swearing not to say anything else ridiculous tonight.

'The folly of youth,' he commented, taking some caviare for himself.

'I'm nearly twenty-three,' she said defensively.

'A babe in arms.' He studied her, eyes drifting over the lines of her body under the grey velvet gown she was wearing. 'Yet you've got the grace and poise of someone far older. A strange mixture of confidence and naïveté, if you don't mind me saying so.'

'Let's talk about you,' Lana said, deciding it was time to get that searchlight gaze off her.

'Let's dance instead,' he countermanded, taking her hand firmly and getting up.

There was hardly room on the crowded floor for one more couple. The dancing was old-fashioned, cheek-to-cheek, almost intoxicatingly romantic. Philip drew her close with strong, possessive arms as they stepped on to the smooth floor. Her pulses seemed to drown out the music for a second as her senses adjusted to the shock of feeling his big, lean body so close against her skin.

'Why do you come to New York?' she asked, wishing her head wasn't spinning so giddily.

'There's more spare money here than there is in Britain,' he informed her. 'The idea of investing their dollars in Britain is rather new to most American investors. If I can persuade them to invest with us—so that we can re-invest in English industry—I make a crust.'

'Some crust,' she commented, clinging to him in the crush of dancers. 'Don't the American banks get cross with you?'

'Sometimes.' He said it with an expression which said he didn't give a damn about the American banks either way.

'My father says you're a financial genius,' she said with a quirk of her eyebrows to make it almost a challenge. 'Are you?'

'It's all very simple,' he smiled. 'I borrow from the rich and lend to the poor.'

'The Robin Hood of Threadneedle Street,' she commented lightly.

'Indeed.' With a soft harmony of saxophones, the band slid into the bittersweet strains of *I Get Along Without You Very Well*, and he swung her lightly round in his arms. 'You're as light as thistledown,' he said, almost with surprise. 'Where did you learn to dance?'

'My mother taught me when I was just a girl.' She smiled up into the dazzlingly handsome face, swaying to the rhythm in his arms.

'When did she die?' he asked gently.

'I was thirteen.' Her mouth softened. 'She was a truly beautiful woman, Philip, like a film-star. Very feminine. Everyone adored her—she and my father were always going out, dancing, wining and dining ... She had the loveliest clothes you can imagine—I'll always associate lace and silk with her.' She smiled. 'I suppose it was through her that I came to love fashion. She taught me so many things—dancing was only one of them. Trouble is, most men who take me out dancing take me to discos, where I can't show off my accomplishments!'

'Your accomplishments are being appreciated tonight,' he said with a glint. He brushed her hair with his lips, almost accidentally. 'In fact, you're rather more accomplished than I imagined.'

She looked up at him again, her hair falling in a golden wave down her naked back. 'Did you think I was too young when you first met me?' she smiled.

'Too young for what?' he enquired drily, eyes still holding that private amusement—was it at her expense?

'Too young to be taken seriously. In a business sense, I mean,' she added hastily.

'It's not youth that counts in life. It's will.'

'Hmmm.' She was feeling like she hadn't done in years, happy, relaxed, almost floated off her feet by the spell he cast over her. The soft jazz was earthy, yet it flowed to a delicious rhythm. Philip's presence was powerfully male, the movements of his hard body provocative and reassuring at the same time. She felt a quiver of nerves at the brush of his thigh against hers. 'Tell me,' she commanded, 'isn't it rather unusual for a respectable banker to indulge himself in motor-racing?'

'I don't lay any claims to respectability,' he pointed out gravely. 'Racing gives me an outlet for my aggressions, Lana. It's a strangely simple, pure experience, with none of the complexities of high finance.'

'It gives you an escape?'

'It's——' He hesitated, as though wondering whether she'd understand. 'It's a way of getting back to myself. My inner self. You tend to lose sight of the real values of life when you're in business.' He smiled at her. 'You're still too young to know what I mean, but you'll find out one day how all too easy it is to get so caught up in the daily routine of making money that you forget how good it is to be alive.'

'Do you really have to risk your life in a fast car to make it worthwhile?' she asked sceptically.

'That's an odd question, coming from someone who's just bought herself a Porsche!'

'I bought the Porsche because of its beauty,' she said primly, 'not to go racing in. I mean, you could just go for a walk in the country and look up at the sky. That would remind you how sweet life is, wouldn't it?'

'Or I could make love to a beautiful woman,' he said softly, eyes on hers. 'Yes, if I cared enough for the woman it would have the same effect for both of us. But there's something about danger which concentrates the mind wonderfully.'

'I'll bet.' He was a complex man, she was thinking, not an easy man to know or get near to. But he had a serious, adult quality that almost frightened her. The men she'd known before him had all been boys, really. This one was a man, a real man. He was like a giant magnet, pulling her towards him. It would be so very easy to fall under this man's spell! 'Yet if I was your wife, Philip, I don't think I'd be able to bear your racing.'

'But you're not my wife,' he grinned. 'As a matter of fact, I'm racing on Saturday, here at the

New York track, for the American touring car championship. Why not come and watch me win?'

'I might,' she said cautiously. 'But I don't know much about motor sport,' she went on with a little shrug. 'I'm afraid it tends to bore me.'

'*Chacun à son goût,*' he smiled, unoffended. 'It's up to you.'

'Merchant banking must be intolerably dull,' she suggested, changing pace absent-mindedly as the band eased into *Blue of Blue*, 'I mean, after motor-racing, and what not, counting money all day can't exactly be thrilling.'

'On the contrary,' he said, green eyes glinting. 'Merchant banking is the most exciting thing I've done to date. We don't simply invest people's money in stocks and bonds, Lana. We finance businesses, help them to grow and flourish. As I hope to do with you.' He ran his fingers along her bare shoulders, making her shiver involuntarily. 'A client will approach us with nothing more than a brilliant notion,' he went on. 'If we think there's merit in the man or the idea, or both, we'll make it all come true. There's nothing quite like the feeling of seeing projects come to life under your hands, growing from little more than a few words on a piece of paper to a living, growing structure.'

'All through the magic of money,' Lana commented, deliberately provocative to try and attack his potent self-assurance.

'You can't do very much without money,' he replied, laughter-lines creasing at the corners of his eyes. 'Come on, let's sit down before you wear me out.'

Some chance of *that*, she thought wryly as they made their way back to the table.

'I don't just count notes all day,' he said,

pouring her a foaming glass of champagne. 'I back
people the high street banks wouldn't touch with a
barge-pole. Last month I flew down to Bermuda
to scuba-dive on an eighteenth-century treasure
wreck. For two years we've been financing a man
called Charles Delafaye while he looked for it. He
was sure it was there somewhere, and I was sure he
was right. He's found it at last, and now we're
financing him while he recovers about two tons of
gold, silver, and precious stones from the coral
reefs.'

'Wow,' Lana said, impressed against her will.

'A few months back I was up in Alaska,' he
went on. 'We're financing oil-exploration in the
frozen wasteland. As soon as I got back to
England I had to drive out to Newmarket to see
a million-dollar stud racehorse a consortium of
businessmen wanted to buy. We've just bought
several buildings right here, in Wall Street. With
property prices the way they are in Manhattan,
that isn't bad going for a private bank. In the
same day once I visited a perfume factory we'd
set up in Devon, and a man who keeps six
thousand pigs in Cornwall. All financed by
London Corporate. No, Lana, it isn't exactly
dull.'

'I guess not,' she admitted, wide-eyed. It was
easier now to see how he'd kept that hard, tanned
look. And why he moved and spoke with such sure
confidence. 'I must seem like very small fry to
you.'

'Projects are interesting because of their intrinsic
worth,' he said silkily. 'Not because of their size.
It's people who're interesting, Lana. Not money.
Banking's about people—at least my kind of
banking is.' He glanced at his watch. 'It's one a.m.

I don't want to be responsible for putting rings under those beautiful eyes. Let's go.'

At the door of her apartment, Lana turned to him, feeling strangely shy suddenly. 'I've enjoyed tonight, Philip.'

'Rather more than you expected to?' he suggested with a quirk of one eyebrow.

'I didn't say that,' she said hastily.

He smiled. 'And I didn't seduce you after all, did I?'

'N-no,' she agreed, flushing.

'Good night, Lana,' he said softly. 'I'll be in touch soon.' His kiss was firm against her mouth, but it didn't linger. 'I enjoyed getting to know you, too.' Then he was gone.

Lana let herself into her apartment, her heart pounding. She still felt high, the champagne fizzing in her blood. Was he going to ask her out again? Yes, she prayed, yes, let him! She danced through to her bedroom, hugging herself, remembering the intoxicating feel of Philip's arms as they'd danced. When she'd gone out to meet Philip for the first time, she hadn't dreamed that things would turn out like this ... He excited her more than she'd believed possible; being with him gave her an inkling of just how overwhelming a relationship with a man could be.

Up till now she'd thought of love as a comfortable kind of friendship that would take second place to work. But no one who loved Philip Casson could possibly put him second to *anything*. He was just too important, too powerful a presence. He would dominate, sweep you off your feet. He was almost dangerous because of that very quality. She couldn't help wondering how many women had loved him, what they'd felt, what had happened to them. It would take someone very special indeed, she knew that, to hold him. There must be a lot of broken hearts behind him. A lot.

But over the next few days she had to put all frivolities aside as she worked on the collection of evening gowns for Susanna Nardi on Fifth Avenue. When she'd started her course in Chicago three years ago, Lana had dreamed that one day her designs would be on sale at Susanna Nardi on New York's most glittering fashion boulevard. Now it was coming true.

The ideas she had in mind were exciting, but difficult to work with. She'd wanted to get right back to the idea of 'the little cocktail dress', the acme of elegance expressed in the minimum of line and material, but it was so hard not to be hackneyed or derivative. The research and ceaseless redesigning kept her fully occupied.

On Wednesday morning, Michael Signa telephoned to say that American Fashions were going to use every design she'd given them. He was amusing and bright, but Philip Casson had rather spoiled her for men who were simply amusing, and she was glad to get away from his ceaseless talk.

When she took her designs in to Nardi on Fifth Avenue on Friday morning, Erica Gilbert, the chief buyer, was visibly delighted. 'Perfect, Lana, just perfect!' She held up the detailed drawing of a shimmering violet gown she'd been examining. 'These little dresses are sensational, Lana. Completely against this year's trend so far, but so original. Susanna will love them.' She looked at Lana with clever brown eyes. 'The inspiration was Paris, right?'

'Yes,' Lana nodded.

'But you've made it all your own. I'm going to have these made up by Mrs Jameson, our top tailor. They'll come out beautifully, I promise you. Can she ring you if she needs to know anything?'

'Of course.'

'When they're ready, I'll put them on display with a new range of leather that's just come in from an Italian designer, and maybe some of the handmade jewellery from Merak. Come in and take a peek in a fortnight or so.' The fashion buyer picked up another design, this time in contrasting salmon and ivory silk. 'There's a freshness about this work that really appeals to me. It's so adaptable, so free of quirkiness.' Her face was friendly as she handed Lana the cheque she'd just written out. 'Come in soon, and see what we've done with your patterns, okay?'

'I will,' Lana promised. As they walked through the softly-lit shop-floor to the exit, Lana looked around her. Shopping here was an exquisite, if expensive, experience. Nardi had always seemed a kind of shrine to her. Now she realised that it was a living, bustling thing, for ever changing and adapting. It was a good feeling to be part of it, to think that she was contributing, in her own small way, to the kind of culture that high fashion represented.

When she got back to her apartment, there was a note awaiting her.

'I'd like you to see the results of my study. If you're free tomorrow afternoon, call my office and ask my secretary to make an appointment. 439, Morgan Towers, East 79th Street.

Philip Casson.'

As she waited nervously in the anteroom to

Philip's office, Lana reflected that the New York office of the London Corporate Bank obviously ran like clockwork. Or rather, like the computerised digital clock that was pulsing on the wall over the switchboard.

This was the other side of Philip's personality. The efficient ruthlessness which enabled him to succeed brilliantly in an environment that could dwarf the human element, belittling you in its maze of chromed steel and tinted glass.

As an artist, she couldn't help feeling slightly lost sometimes, a little awed by all this mechanised efficiency. She knew that she'd never achieve the kind of razor-edged precision which people like Philip Casson could call into play. It simply wasn't her. On the other hand, it was very reassuring to have it working on her behalf!

But she didn't want him to take her for an empty-head. That morning she'd had her hair cut into one of the soft, feminine styles that were becoming fashionable in New York for the autumn. The neat black suit, she hoped, conveyed the right note of businesslike sobriety.

Covertly, she studied the secretary behind the desk, and decided that she was a typical product of ultra-neat, ultra-modern New York—immaculately groomed and coiffured, answering a ceaseless flow of incoming calls with a discreetly murmuring mauve mouth. The pulse on the clock was now showing 2:00 p.m., and precisely on cue, the secretary smiled lightly at Lana.

'Please go through,' she said. 'Mr Casson is free now.'

The moment of truth had come. Expectant and edgy she walked through. Philip was writing at a massive desk as she came in, but as the door clicked shut behind her, he looked up, and slid the golden pen back into its sheath.

'Hello, Lana,' he greeted her, smiling with his eyes as he ushered her in. 'I like your hair.' The dove-grey carpet was soft underfoot as Lana walked slowly through. She hadn't been prepared for the richness of the place. It was beautiful, extravagant. White linen furniture, baroque paintings, exquisitely-chosen antiques. Only the computers arrayed in an alcove suggested a more purposeful side to the apartment.

And New York wasn't kept out of the mood, either; one wall was a window that looked out on to the canyons and chasms of the skyscraper city all around, now tinted crimson by the setting sun.

'This is beautiful,' she couldn't help saying. 'Ravishing!'

He had the intercom in his hand. 'No interruptions for the time being, Bridgit.' He turned to Lana, replacing the instrument. 'I'm pleased you like it. It's had more effort put into it than most city offices—but then, I live here. My own suite is just through that archway. When the new branch office opens at the beginning of next year, I'll convert this place back into a home.' He waved her to a chair.

The three-piece suit in charcoal silk was ultra-formal, yet it could no more disguise his raw masculinity than the bathing-slip he'd worn at their first meeting. If anything, the beautifully-cut clothes added to his already massive powers of magnetism. He must have a stunning wardrobe, she realised.

'Will you have a martini?'

'If I didn't know better, I'd suspect you of trying

to keep me drunk,' she smiled. 'I'd love one.' She
couldn't keep the anxious question back any
longer. 'Well—is it on or not?'

In answer, Philip dropped a slim folder in her
lap, then went to the drinks cabinet.

'That's the costing exercise I did,' he said,
emptying the cocktail shaker into two glasses.
'Based on what you told me, and some figures
given me by some friends in the rag trade, I made
some estimates. See what you think.'

She took the three or four sheets of paper out of
the folder and read through them rapidly. They
contained a remarkably concise account of how
the workshop could be set up, and what it would
cost. The lists of figures and planning details were
a lot fuller than she'd expected. He'd done some
serious research, that was obvious, and the
projections he'd made were, if anything, conservative. The concluding sentences made it clear
that, in his opinion, the project was definitely on:
'Providing the essentials of low overheads and a
compact unit are kept to, the project should realise
considerable profits.'

If she could produce the goods, it was obvious,
there was nothing to stop the business from
becoming a runaway success.

Depending on two things. Philip's continued
backing, and her continued inspiration.

'To answer your question,' he said, passing her a
glass, 'it appears to be a quite viable proposition.
You should be making a profit from the very first
months, which will enable you to pay off your
capital loan and build up some reserves. And if
you become as successful as you so obviously
deserve to be, you ought to make a tidy fortune
within a few years.'

So! Lana looked up at him hesitantly. There was no laughter in his handsome face. 'You really have that much confidence in me?' she asked.

He stood with one fist on his hip, tall and dark, looking more like a Red Indian prince than a respectable merchant banker. 'Of course. You could set up a workshop in no time at all. You'd need a single large loan to cover the machinery, which you'd most likely have to buy, rather than lease. Then you'd need a running account to cover the week-to-week costs such as materials, services, the rent on your premises for a year or so, and the salaries of your staff. Perhaps the best way to run it would be in the form of a business account with the Bank. You'd use special cheques for all purchases or payments to do with the business. Of course, you'd have complete discretion over whatever you did.' He raised his glass to her, and drank.

Feeling slightly bemused, Lana followed suit. The cocktail was velvety-smooth, intoxicating.

'You'd pay for all that?' she blinked, turning back to the file. It was far, far more than she'd ever expected or anticipated. 'You really do mean it?'

'I wouldn't have wasted time on it if I didn't mean it,' he retorted. 'I told you the other night, Lana, setting up businesses is my business. That's what merchant banking is all about. I supply the capital, the expertise, a solid backing. You'd be free to create.'

'But still——' She laughed uncomfortably, still unable to fully believe it. 'These figures—what if I can't match them? How on earth could you be sure you'd get your money back?'

'I trust you,' he said, watching the hesitant

excitement in her face. 'You've got what it takes, Lana. I'd bet on that. You were born for success. I can help you get there a lot quicker.'

'I have to admit I'm taken aback,' she said, shaking her head. 'I never expected you to go this far, Philip.'

He sat down opposite her, a dark, potent figure with an amused expression.

'So—what do you think?'

'I think it's wonderful,' she sighed, breaking into a smile. She laid the folder aside, and leaned back. 'I just find it hard to believe that my little affairs count for very much in your huge corporation.'

He rose, fluid and lithe, and poured them fresh drinks. 'London Corporate isn't huge,' he smiled. 'It's just exclusive.'

'Do you have to wear the right tie to open an account?' she asked.

'Something like that. A lot of our clients are titled, for example. They like banking in a Grade One listed Georgian building. Saves their lordships from having to queue up in Lloyd's or Barclay's like the rest of the world.'

'You sound rather cynical,' Lana observed, almost smiling. 'Most bank managers are such solemn people.'

'Agreed. If I ever found myself turning out like that, I'd change jobs.'

'I don't think there's much danger of that,' she told him, watching him from under her lashes. The laughter-lines around those shockingly direct eyes, North Sea green flecked with gold, somehow warmed you inside. Like sunlight breaking into a cold room. You had to keep reminding yourself of the explosive, possibly destructive power that lay in the iron-hard muscles under the velvet skin.

'I don't think so, either,' he agreed. 'By the way—remember that wreck I told you about—the one in Bermuda?'

'Of course.'

He took something out of an ormolu box on the coffee-table, and tossed it over to her. It landed in her lap with surprising heaviness for its size. 'I found that while I was diving last month.'

She held the broad, solid coin in her palm. Pure gold, gleaming and untarnished after its centuries under the sea. He watched her face as she marvelled over the beautiful thing, the date under the intricate cross reading 1727.

'It's a Spanish *piastre*,' he told her in his soft, deep voice. 'What the old sailors called a piece of eight.'

'Like in *Treasure Island*?' she asked wonderingly.

'Like in *Treasure Island*. Living proof that merchant banking isn't dull.'

'It's absolutely beautiful!'

She rubbed the smooth coin with her thumb, lost in its mellow richness.

He glanced at the gold watch on his wrist. 'I'm afraid that I have clients to meet in a short while,' he informed her. He had an easy knack, she reflected unhappily, of telling you when you were no longer wanted! She prepared to leave. 'I'd like you to read over my estimates and see what you think,' he went on. 'It would also be sensible to discuss the idea with your father.'

'I'll do that,' she promised.

'And then we can work out the final details. Over dinner, perhaps?'

The invitation spread a warm feeling through

her stomach. 'Whenever you like,' she said, a little breathless.

'Friday night, then?'

'Fine,' she nodded, ridiculously happy.

'I'm racing the next morning,' he said, showing her to the door. 'It'll do me good to be able to relax the night before.'

'I'll do my best to entertain,' she smiled. She held out the coin. 'Here's your piece of eight.'

He looked at it, then smiled directly into her eyes, leaving her suddenly weak at the knees. 'You keep it.'

'You're joking,' she said in disbelief, offering it to him again.

'I'm not joking. It's yours.'

'But I *couldn't*,' she gasped, staring from his face to the golden disc in her palm.

'I found it among the coral,' he said. 'It was a gift from the sea to me. Now I'm giving it to you.'

'Philip,' she said, at a complete loss for words, 'I don't—I don't know what to say. It must be worth a fortune!'

'A couple of hundred dollars. Will it buy me a kiss?' he asked, his eyes glowing sunlit green at her discomfiture.

'A—a kiss?'

He leaned down and drew her close while she was still opening her mouth to stammer. His lips were warm, firm, like the kiss of the sun on naked skin. Overwhelmed by him, Lana froze, her senses stunned. She could smell the aftershave on his skin, feel his man's body hard and powerful against her own.

Then the shock wore off, and she pushed away from him shakily, her lips clinging to his as though they couldn't bear to be separated. The intensity of her own reaction frightened her.

Confusion made her head spin dizzily. This had started out as a game, but she was losing control, her emotions developing a lot faster than she wanted them to!

'I don't think that was very sensible,' she said in an unsteady voice, her face pale. 'This is supposed to be a business relationship, Philip!'

'Don't be such a prig,' he purred, eyes watching her mouth as though he were imminently contemplating a repeat performance.

'I'm not a prig,' she said stiffly, and turned away, her breasts and stomach aching, her whole body trembling with the feelings he awoke in her. It might be amusing to him, but it stirred deep feelings in her, feelings she didn't want abused. 'But that kiss was a lot too—intimate—for such a short acquaintance.'

'Kissing is an excellent way to improve an acquaintance,' he said with a husky laugh. 'And you can't deny that it was rather delicious.'

'That isn't the point.' It was an effort for her to face those glowing eyes again. She knew a lot less about men than she'd admitted to herself up till now, and even less about her own self. If he knew just how weak and giddy she felt, she'd be finished! 'You'd better take your piece of eight,' she said quietly, holding the coin out to him. She'd been clenching it so tight that it had cut a half-moon in her palm. 'It doesn't buy you that kind of liberty.'

His mouth quirked in a wry smile. 'Now you are being a prig. Keep it as a pledge against my good behaviour on Friday. Shall we say around eight?'

What was she to do about this relationship that was snowballing so swiftly into something overwhelmingly important? If she were to admit the truth to herself, she was becoming far more fascinated with Philip Casson himself than with any financial help he might be able to give her. She'd once danced for joy at the thought of setting up her own business. Now it was Philip who altered her moods, putting her through emotional hoops as easily as though he knew every secret of her heart.

'Around eight,' she repeated dully. Feeling that she'd like to sit down for a long while, Lana nodded dumbly, and let him escort her out.

She hadn't been kissed like that before. Not with such confidence, with such erotic expertise. And the golden coin? That was no trinket, for all it had been given with apparent casualness. What did it promise? A fulfilment she could only dream of?

Philip Casson had the ability to melt the very bones inside you. He'd obviously loved a lot of women; could he possibly have a serious interest in her?

He thrilled her to the core—and yet he could also be strangely upsetting. Philip was a devastatingly attractive man, and none of the fumbling experiences she'd had with boys before now could have prepared her to deal with him, with his will and formidable purpose. Her feelings were turbulent and mixed, and the prospect of dining with him on Friday wasn't nearly as pleasant a prospect as it had seemed before the velvety contact of those male lips.

The very first time she'd met him, he'd struck her as a man who could be callous towards women, using them and discarding them. The sort of man who preferred brief affairs, yet who had the power to make women love him. Was that true? The thought was painful enough to give her a dire warning that she was growing a lot more interested in Philip than was good for her—or her untried heart.

Yet he drew her so powerfully.

The coin was so precious that she wanted it always with her. She took it to a 47th Street jeweller as soon as she got a spare moment, and asked him to set it into a simple pendant to hang round her neck.

'This thing's valuable,' he said, studying the coin covetously. 'One of the best I've seen—you'd think it had just come out of the sea. Care to sell? I'll give you a good price.'

'No, thanks. It was a gift. A special one.'

'I'll say it was special,' the little balding man agreed emphatically. 'He must be one hell of a guy. Okay, it'll be ready by Saturday.'

'Couldn't you make it Friday?' she pleaded, thinking of her date with Philip.

'Saturday, Friday, what difference does it make?' He relented. 'Okay. Call by Friday afternoon, and I'll have it ready for you then.'

She'd promised to lunch with May Baragli on Wednesday, so she walked to the end of the avenue at noon, and descended into the subway. In the graffiti-scrawled wasteland below she sat thinking. Four million New Yorkers used the system every day, but it was still the loneliest place in the world. So many faces, so many people, so little human contact.

'Have you met The Lord?'

With a start, Lana looked into the crazy eyes of the old lady beside her. 'I beg your pardon?'

'He's watching you,' the old lady said, grabbing

Lana's slender arm in a claw-like hand. 'Watching you right now, young lady. And when he catches aholt of you, you can kick and you can holler and you can squirm, but he ain't gonna let you go!'

This town was full of mad people, Lana thought with a shudder, freeing herself from the grasping fingers as the train pulled into Prospect Park station, her stop.

'He ain't *never* gonna let you go,' the old witch called after her.

She hurried from the subway exit towards May's house, the wind flattening her clothes against her firm breasts, revealing the taut lines of her thighs. Maybe she should run, now, while the going was good, before Philip hurt her. Maybe the way to get him out of her blood was to try and get back to a formal business relationship. Treat him as a partner, nothing more. Tell herself he was only her banker. And behave accordingly towards him.

May's place in Brooklyn was a lot different from her own flat in the smarter part of the old West Side. The area was shabby, poor, criss-crossed by desolate streets in which abandoned and gutted buildings stood side by side with rows of brownstones and mean-looking stores. May's street was prettier, with real trees on the sidewalks, and children playing on the steps and railings that led up to each front door. The distant skyscrapers of Manhattan made an odd contrast, rising above the drab Victorian rooftops.

'Hi there!' It was a tonic to see May's round, brown face beaming at her from the doorway. 'Come on in.'

May had been a good friend to Lana at the fashion school in Chicago. Not everyone had liked the English blonde who wasn't just beautiful and hard-working, but was also talented. It was typical of May that there wasn't the slightest trace of jealousy in her, not even now, when after graduation Lana had gone straight into freelance work, landing some of the most exciting jobs going, while May had had to settle for well-paid but boring hack-work for a mail-order company.

A lot of people at the Chicago College of Design, maybe less perceptive than May Baragli, had decided that Lana's famous poise was simply arrogance, especially those men who'd been rebuffed by her. But May had seen straight through to the inherent sweetness in Lana's character, and had realised instinctively that her coolness was only a mask for shyness and reserve, the rapid adulthood that comes to all young people who lose one or both parents.

May's Italian cooking, as usual, was superb, and after a glass of the ruby-red wine, Lana felt her spirits lifting.

'Delicious,' she complimented, and sipped the wine, savouring its rough sweetness on her tongue. 'You can taste the summer in this Chianti.'

May picked up the bottle and studied the label musingly.

'Orvieto. That's where it comes from. I went back there with my parents when I was sixteen, you know. They came from a little village not far from the town.' She sighed, pouring the rest of the wine into their glasses. 'Tuscany is so beautiful, Lana. You'd love it there.'

'I'll bet I would,' Lana said feelingly. 'When we're rich and famous, we'll both go.'

'You'll be rich and famous a long time before me,' May smiled, serving them with more *lasagne*. 'Tell me all about your divine merchant banker!'

Hesitantly, Lana told May the whole story. But she didn't mention the golden piece of eight that Philip had given her. Somehow, that had been too precious, too private to talk about. 'I'm having dinner with him on Friday,' she concluded, pulling a little face. 'We'll probably finalise the arrangements then.'

May considered her friend's drooping mouth. 'If I was on the brink of a glorious new career,' she commented, 'I'd be looking a bit happier about it!'

'I *am* happy,' Lana said moodily.

'He sounds charming.' May cocked her head, her bright brown eyes bird-like. 'If a little intimidating. Is he?'

'Yes to both.' Lana stared into her wine, thinking of the glossy, dark hair, the way his eyes always seemed to laugh at her. 'He upsets me.'

'He *upsets* you?' May had to laugh. 'What kind of comment is that?'

'He kissed me the last time we met,' Lana said, fidgeting with her glass.

'That's it?' May was still smiling. 'So. What sort of kiss? Cheek? Lips? Friendly? Romantic?'

'On the lips,' Lana sighed. 'And upsetting.'

'He was probably just feeling fatherly—he's a friend of your father's, isn't he?'

'Yes. But he's much younger than Dad,' she added quickly.

Judging that Lana wasn't going to finish her pasta, May rose and started clearing the plates. 'He's still way older than you are. And he probably already has a lot on his plate from the romantic point of view, anyway. You'd barely make an *hors d'oeuvre* for a man like that. I wouldn't worry about him.'

'I'm not worried about *him*,' Lana said meaningfully.

'Don't tell me the well-known Fox coolth is beginning to thaw,' May derided from the kitchen. 'That would be the best news I'd had in years!'

'Oh?' Lana followed her in with the knives and forks. 'Why?'

'You had to study hard at college, we all did. There just wasn't the time for fooling around, not if someone was headed for the top—as you definitely were. Besides, we were all just kids.' May put the plates in the sink, and pushed Lana firmly back into the tiny dining-room, sitting her down and facing her. 'But now? You're a grown woman, Lana. It's time you started taking men seriously—especially men like Philip, if you really think he's interested in you.'

'Maybe *I'm* not that interested,' Lana muttered.

'And maybe pigs can fly,' May retorted. 'You're always trying to be so cool. The way you talk about men—as though they were all just pathetic fools there for you to exploit! One day someone like Philip Casson is going to let you down with a jolt.'

'I can take care of myself,' Lana said, smiling slightly at May's earnestness. 'I'm a career-girl for the time being, and I'm not going to let Philip distract me from that. Things have gone far enough,' she decided.

'Listen,' May said, patting Lana's knee, 'someday you're going to discover that there's a hell of a lot more to life than a career—like a man!'

'Hah!' But the words struck a chill. Philip *was* endangering her dedication to her career. It wasn't that her work didn't fulfil her any more—she couldn't imagine not being excited about designing

new and exciting clothes. But she'd somehow lost
her awe of the fashion world, and had begun to see
the fragility of so much of it. Fashions came and
fashions went. The speed with which today's latest
lines became back numbers was just a little
frightening.

It made her feel that her life wasn't full. That
there was an empty place in it. Dangerous feelings
for an up-and-coming designer!

'It's not too late to change the way I feel about
Philip,' she said, almost to herself. 'Before the rot
really sets in!'

'What are you going to do?' May asked
ironically.

'I'm going to tone the whole relationship down
from now on,' she said decisively.

'You mean, turn Philip off, like a radio?'

'Something like that.'

May grinned mirthlessly. 'Good luck, kid.
You're going to need it.'

CHAPTER FOUR

ON Friday evening, Lana sat naked on her bed,
blow-drying her hair into windswept waves of
gold, her mind full of thoughts about the evening
ahead. Her body had long since lost the deep tan
she'd acquired sailing on Lake Michigan while
she'd been a student, but her figure was as trim
and neat as it had ever been. Standing up, she
looked at herself in the mirror.

Did she really have the kind of voluptuous
curves men wanted? Her breasts were high and

firm, but she'd always believed men preferred
fuller busts. Something to get hold of, she
supposed with a little smile.

She turned, hands on her hips, studying herself.
The fine muscles of her back and stomach were
well-defined under the smooth skin. Was she too
trim and boyish to be womanly? Maybe. Still, she
was almost flawless, her colours honey and gold.

She had collected the pendant from the jeweller
that afternoon, and he'd made a fine job. The
heavy piece of eight gleamed against the silky skin
between her breasts, inviting wanton comparison
to the perfect discs of her nipples. On its simple
gold chain, it was beautiful, almost masculine. It
somehow made her body look more delicate.

She settled on a deceptively simple evening
gown, pale green silk with a plunging back and
neckline that made gentle fun of her undramatic
bust. The colour and the lines suited her well,
giving depth to her colouring and flattering the
lithe quality of her figure. High heeled sandals in a
matching green raised her a couple of inches, so
that she wouldn't be too small beside him.

Looking in the mirror again, she sighed. An
English dog-rose, tarted up to look like an exotic
hybrid.

'You look like a blonde Minnie Mouse,' she told
herself sadly.

Through her high window she watched Philip
arrive in his silver Jaguar at eight, dazzlingly
handsome in an evening jacket. Whatever he wore,
she reflected, could never conceal the thrusting,
aggressive quality of his manhood. Nor could it
conceal his devastating magnetism, the attraction
that would always make any woman's head turn.

Nerves were fluttering in her stomach as she

opened the door to him, and tried a shaky smile. Toning down the relationship was going to be a task for a very much braver Lana than she was right now!

'Well well,' he said in his husky voice. His eyes were on the piece of eight at her breast. 'That looks rather delicious on you.'

'I—I had it set on a chain,' she faltered.

'So I see.' He touched the coin, then looked into her eyes. 'I'm glad. It looks better on you than it did on the sea-bed.'

The intensity of his gaze made her mouth go dry, her stomach contracting with nerves. She dropped her eyes, tugging restlessly at the coin. 'You said it was a token of your good behaviour,' she said in a small voice.

He laughed gently and took her arm with as much grace as though she'd been a queen. 'We'll see about that,' he said obliquely. 'Shall we go?'

The old Gershwin melodies the band were playing fitted very sweetly into her mood right now.

Lana gazed dreamily past the lanterns to where the lights of fishing boats glimmered on Long Island Sound. The meal had been exquisite—Blue Point Oysters, clams on the half-shell, succulent lobster Thermidor and Nova Scotia salmon; salads, a fragrant California white to wash it all down with; and to conclude, a blazing ice-cream *bombe* that had made her feel as pampered as a Russian Princess. How could you tone down your feelings towards a man who fed you ice-cream *bombe*?

'And to think people imagine the American cuisine consists of hamburgers and Coke,' she sighed. Philip smiled at her contented expression.

'I hope you aren't going to get fat through me.'

'I'll risk it.'

'Perhaps I ought to exercise you,' he decided. She followed him on to the dance-floor, and they swayed to the gentle rhythms for a while, holding each other close. She'd discovered that if she held her doubts and worries down, she could dream herself into a blissful fantasy world in which nothing could happen to her.

And it was heaven to dance with him, to feel the slow eroticism of his body moving against hers— the civilised, elegant eroticism of dancing.

It was cool enough for them to wander out on to the verandah overlooking the bay, and to stand against the rail, arm in arm, looking out across the dancing lights.

'I wish you were always like you are tonight,' he said quietly. 'Happy, gay. Not trying to stand on your dignity like some dowager duchess of ninety.'

'Oh.' Feeling slightly foolish, she glanced at him. 'Am I really like that?'

'Sometimes.' He was laughing now, his eyes glinting grey-green.

'I showed your figures to my father,' she told him, changing the subject.

'Indeed.' His mouth caressed the sensitive skin of her temple, inviting her to want him with that sweet, sharp ache she was coming to know so well. 'What did he say?'

'He said it all sounded wonderful,' she said, feeling dizzy with the nearness of him.

'And you? What do you think of our proposed—partnership?'

'I'm still not sure that I'm not dreaming it all,' she answered, slightly nervous. 'Can it really work the way you describe it?'

'Easily. It won't take you more than a month or two to rent some kind of premises, buy some basic machinery, and hire staff. I'll have one of our experts advise you on setting everything up, so that you get all the details right from the start. Problems like tax and accounting have ruined many a promising company. When you're well into the swing of production, we can start the publicity rolling. A couple of television interviews, articles in the papers, a nice big colour spread in some glossy magazine.'

'You can arrange all those things?' she asked in awe.

'Naturally,' he smiled.

She didn't answer, just clung to him, wishing to God she had a crystal ball to see into the future, so that she could know what part in her life Philip Casson was destined to play.

'How on earth can you trust me?' she wondered.

'We fit,' he said in his quiet growl, as though that were answer enough. 'Don't you feel it?' His fingers stroked the smooth skin of her neck, trailing down her spine to make her shiver with pleasure. 'We're going to make fabulous partners.'

'But what will you want in return? Banks don't operate for charity.'

'There would be certain conditions attached,' he said.

'What conditions?'

'Let's discuss that on the way home, shall we?' he smiled.

'But I want to discuss them *now*!'

'Then we'll go home now,' he said with incontrovertible logic. 'It's getting late for working girls, anyway.'

'But I'm having such a wonderful time!' she groaned.

'And I have a race to run tomorrow.'

'Your race.' She looked up at him, eyes remorseful. 'I'd forgotten all about your race! You'll have to get your sleep. Come on.'

Somehow, the intimacy of the evening had been shattered by the prospect of the next day's race. She hadn't thought about it much, but now it rather chilled her.

'Tell me,' she demanded, clinging to his arm as they walked out to the car ten minutes later, 'just how dangerous is it really?'

'Just dangerous enough to be interesting,' he smiled. 'Which is what makes it fun.'

'But not so much fun for people who care about you,' she said sharply. He looked at her, but didn't comment.

'Are there ever accidents?' she asked as she climbed into the leather-and-walnut interior of the Jaguar beside him.

'Not often.' He eased the powerful car out of the crowded car-park. 'Have you decided whether you're coming yet?'

'I'm not sure if I could stand it,' she said gloomily.

'You mean the thought of losing your loan?' he teased, mocking her with green wolf's eyes.

'You know exactly what I mean,' she retorted, looking away.

'My sponsors have a special trailer at the track,' he went on, still with that amused look on his face. 'Champagne and caviare, right up your street. Bring a friend, and see for yourself what it's like.'

'All right,' she said, nodding. 'I'll do exactly that.'

'Excellent.' He reached into his inside pocket, and took out a plastic card. 'That'll get you into the track. It's only a four-hour race, and it'll all be over by three. You might even enjoy it.'

'I doubt it,' she commented, slipping the card into her bag. She nestled down in her seat and turned her mind back to the subject of her fashion house. 'You said there'd be conditions attached to your helping me set up my studio, Phil. What conditions, exactly?'

'First of all,' he said, 'I would stipulate that you pay the capital loan back, in full, within three years.'

'That's fair enough,' Lana commented, looking at his profile. 'What else?'

'During that period, any funds my bank lends you must go into a joint account in your and my names. Meaning that you won't be able to issue any large cheques without my signature as well.'

'I see.' It didn't take more than a few seconds' thought to realise that that would effectively give him control in any major decisions she made, and involve him in practically every step of the way.

'It's quite usual, Lana. And it's mainly for safety measure. To make sure no one rips you off while you're still inexperienced at dealing with money.'

'Oh.'

'Besides, you wouldn't want to spend too much time on the business side of things. You'd need all your time for designing.' He shifted gear as they crossed the bridge, coming within sight of the glittering towers of Manhattan.

For the next twenty minutes they talked over the details and alternatives until he'd pulled up outside her apartment block.

She turned to him. 'It's been such a wonderful

evening, Philip. Would you——' She hesitated. All
the rest of her plans for the evening had crumbled,
so what the hell? 'Would you care to come up for
a nightcap? Or a cup of coffee?'

He glanced at his watch, then smiled. 'Yes, I
would.'

High in the eyrie of her apartment, Lana
fossicked in the kitchen cupboard for the bottle of
brandy that was the only thing she had to drink.

'I know it's here somewhere,' she muttered. 'It
was a Christmas present from someone—ah.'

She gave him the bottle to pour the drinks, took
hers, and kicked off her sandals, enjoying the feel
of the carpet under her bare soles.

'It's been such a lovely evening,' she sighed. She
didn't want it to end, not now. She walked to the
window, and stared out at the vast cobweb of
diamonds stretching out into the night all around
them. 'I was going to be so cool and distant
tonight,' she said quietly.

'Oh?' he smiled. 'Why?'

A wave of unreality rocked her thoughts. She
hadn't asked for all this to happen to her. Philip
was a meteor, an express train that had exploded
into her life from outside, scattering all the neat
little protocols of her existence. 'You're a million
miles removed from the sort of men I've known up
till now, Philip,' she said slowly. 'Maybe you're
used to—to all this. But I'm not. You make me
feel things I don't want to acknowledge—and
that frightens me.'

'Why should it frighten you?' he asked, coming
to her side. She felt his arm slide round her
shoulders, and leaned against him, closing her
eyes.

'You wouldn't understand,' she murmured. It

was as though some mischievous goddess, looking down into the arrogance and self-sufficiency of her vain little heart, had decided to set a sleek black cat among the pigeons.

And would that goddess, just as callously, take Philip away from her once the fun was over?

The intensity of her own feelings for Philip frightened her. It was all happening too fast, too confusingly. Something would happen to take it all away again, she felt that with a dull foreboding.

She turned to him, her eyes haunted. 'How seriously do you take things?' she asked sharply. 'How seriously do you take me?'

'When you behave like a child,' he smiled, 'I don't take you seriously at all. When you're a woman, I take you very seriously indeed.'

'You mean you care about me?' she challenged, staring into the bright depths of his eyes.

'I'd have thought that was obvious by now,' he said in a soft voice, eyes sultry.

'You're so damned confident,' she sighed, aching for him. 'Do you treat all your mistresses in the same way, Philip?'

His eyes narrowed smokily. 'Mistresses?'

'You must have dozens,' she accused, on the verge of tears.

The harsh planes of his face softened. 'My poor Lana. It's all very strange to you, isn't it?' He drew her close, his mouth taking hers in a slow, lingering kiss that invited her to let all her thoughts sink into nothingness, losing herself in the power of his presence.

She clung to him with trembling arms, wanting him so much it frightened her. Her whole body seemed to be crying out for him, her nerves on fire for his touch.

He whispered her name huskily, then scooped her up as though she'd been as light as a bird, and carried her unprotesting body through the dimly-lit apartment to her bedroom.

He laid her on the bed. She felt like a child, looking up at him with dark green eyes, her hair tumbled in swathes of gold around her face, fear struggling with aching need in her heart.

'You're so lovely,' he breathed, his voice just a ragged sigh. Desire for her had dilated his pupils, making his eyes beautiful, cat-like. He pulled off his jacket and sank down beside her. 'I've been wanting you all night . . .'

Lana opened her arms to him, her heart pounding so hard that she could scarcely breathe. He kissed her hard, his mouth mastering her with almost shocking aggression, as though challenging her to resist him if she dared.

Arching her neck as he kissed her throat hungrily, she felt herself melting, pure physical response sweeping her thoughts away. She ran her fingers through his hair, revelling in the thickness of it, whispering his name. Need for him was a hunger that ran in her blood, forcing her against him. He pulled off his shirt, smiling at her; his body was brown and hard, the texture of his skin like warm silk.

He stroked her cheek, murmuring her name. She lay looking up at him, her eyes dark pools that held only his image. The gleaming power of his broad shoulders and sinewy arms was familiar from her dreams. She wanted so much to believe him!

'I've wanted you so long,' he said, touching the bruised satin of her mouth.

'And I want you.' She caught his hand and laid

her cheek in his palm, closing her eyes. 'Yet we hardly know each other. I don't even know whether you're a good man or a bad one.'

'Does that matter?' he smiled.

'I don't know ...' She laid her hands on his breast, her sensitive fingers tracing the marvel of his body. The muscles were perfect, hard-sculpted under the dark smudge of hair that ran down his flat belly. His nipples were dark, stiff with desire under her palms. Weak and shaking, she caressed the hot skin, thrilling to the pulse of the sinews beneath, her fingers brushing across his chest, the muscular column of his throat, caressing his cheek in a timid, yet bold surrender.

'Ah.' Philip shuddered, eyes taking on a brooding, smoky look that made her melt for him. 'You make me want you so much. With those warm eyes, that sweet face——' He traced the line of her throat, his touch gentle against her fine skin, then touched the richness of her golden hair. 'So beautiful.'

'Not too young?' she asked in a husky whisper.

'Much too young.' He kissed her again, possessively now, his mouth telling her she was his woman, his absolutely. It was a kiss that lingered sweetly, his hands caressing the slim shape of her body under the delicate silk of her gown. Their tongues met, touched, caressed with a heart-stopping passion that made her moan against his lips, desire tightening her stomach-muscles and melting her loins.

'You've got so much to give,' he said, holding her close.

'But is this all there is to it?' she asked in a low voice. 'Desire? No love? Nothing apart from our bodies and what they want?'

'Of course there's more to it,' he smiled. 'Much more. I feel it exactly as much as you, Lana.'

'You care for me?' she pleaded.

'Of course I care.'

'Am I the only one?'

'Don't tell me you can't take a little competition,' he teased.

'Not where you're concerned!' she said fiercely, admitting the truth that was burning inside her.

'And if I told you there wasn't any?'

Lana stared up at the tanned, male face. How many women must have wanted him! He'd have been able to pick and choose all of his life. 'I wouldn't believe you,' she sighed.

'So it's catch-twenty-two,' he replied calmly. Deliberately, he unfastened her gown, exposing her naked breasts, making her shiver helplessly. His face was intent as he traced the curves of her body, his touch wondering, light as a feather. 'I couldn't get over you, the first time I saw you at that poolside,' he said in a soft voice. 'You're so perfect, my love. So beautiful, so desirable.'

He cupped her breasts, taking her nipples into his mouth, his tongue brushing the aroused peaks until she curled in helpless pleasure, her nails digging into his shoulders.

Then he was rolling away from her. Dreamy with what he'd done to her, she reached out to him. 'Phil? What is it?'

'This is all wrong,' he said thickly. 'I keep forgetting that you're merely a child.'

'I'm not,' she gasped in disbelief, her voice shaky with passion. 'I'm not a child, Philip. Look at me!'

'You don't understand.' He shook his head, eyes dark. 'We mustn't do this, Lana.'

'We must!' She clambered over to him, almost in tears, unable to comprehend. 'I need you, don't you know that by now?'

'Hush.' His expression was tight. 'No more.'

'But *why*?' she demanded, fighting against shock and confusion. 'What's happened?'

'What's happened is that I've completely lost my head,' he replied tiredly. 'I'm all keyed up because of tomorrow's race, needing an outlet. It would be so easy to use you—and you're much too young, too inexperienced to make this decision.'

She reached for him, sliding her arms around his naked shoulders, still hoping she could rescue the marvellous thing that had happened between them. 'If this will help you relax, it's what I want, too,' she said softly.

He turned to her, holding her gently in his arms. A wry smile etched itself across his mouth. 'Sex isn't a tranquilliser, Lana.'

She took a deep, trembling breath, groping for the words. 'Philip, I'm quite adult enough to make this decision, as you call it.' It was humiliating to beg him to make love to her. God, what pride-denting irony. And she'd been wanting to be cool to *him*! Now she wanted him so badly, wanted him the way only a woman in love can want. She looked into the deep green eyes. 'Have I said something to upset you?'

'No.' He touched her cheek. 'No. I've just upset myself. I thought I had better control over my emotions. You do something to me, Lana. Make me mindless with need.'

'That's exactly what you do to me,' she said desperately.

'You don't understand,' he said gently. 'How could you?'

'Oh, Phil,' she said in an unsteady voice, 'this is a hell of a way to end a beautiful evening.'

'I know.' But he was already rising and pulling his shirt on, his face set.

His eyes met hers, stormy with inner passion. 'I feel exactly the way you do, my love.' The magnetism between them was so strong for a second that it seemed to tear at her very heart. She almost thought he would come to her again; and then, with a wrenching effort, he shook his head, and slung his jacket over his shoulders. 'I go a little crazy before each race. It was completely irresponsible to try and make love to you.'

She turned her face to the pillow. The irony was so painful! She'd tried to be rational about her need for Philip, right from the start. Except that now she was no longer an adolescent, inexperienced and ignorant of herself. She was a woman, aflame with longing for a man she intensely needed. And now it was he who'd terminated the contact between their souls.

Feeling utterly naked and alone, she sat up, pulling her crumpled gown to her, and covered herself with it, and tried desperately not to give way to the pain inside her.

'Little love.' He stooped to kiss her mouth. Her lips clung to his like bruised rose-petals, and she felt him hesitate for an instant before he drew back. 'There'll be other times,' he promised huskily. 'Other times and other places, when we won't have to stop. Believe me?' She nodded mutely, adoring him. 'Good. Will I see you at the track tomorrow?'

'Of—of course.' She tried to say she wouldn't have missed it for worlds, but her throat was too dry. It was cruel to be left like this, poised on the barbed-wire of her love for him . . .

After he'd left, she went to the window, a slim statue in the silvery light. It was such a strange, strange feeling. Frustrated and aching, yet at the same time trembling with joy. She'd never let a man affect her in this way.

She knew she *was* involved with him now. There simply wasn't any choice for her, even if she hadn't wanted it. Philip Casson represented some kind of destiny for her, and sooner or later she was going to have to face that fact fully.

Saturday dawned rainy and grey. Lana called May with Philip's invitation that they both watch the race from his trailer, to which May excitedly agreed.

By ten, Lana was parking the Porsche in the sea of cars outside the track, and they were joining the thirty thousand other spectators around the twisting circuit, overlooked by the towers of Manhattan.

Philip's card secured them instant entrance through the mesh gates marked OFFICIALS. Despite the weather, the atmosphere was one of nervous excitement, almost carnival. The silver Dunlop airship hung high over the track; suspended underneath was the cabin containing live television broadcast units.

As they made their way towards the pits, the public address system was alternating race announcements with amplified hard rock, and the crowds were streaming towards the covered stands or the grassy banks along the three-mile track, in preparation for the start of the race in forty minutes. Shiny umbrellas and raincoats glistened everywhere.

'I bet this is what those old Roman games were like,' May commented breathlessly as they were jostled in the crowd. 'Everyone very jolly at the prospect of a little blood.'

'Don't say that,' Lana groaned, thinking of Philip with a twist of nerves.

They found the trailer, set back from the organised chaos of the pits. Philip was in the luxurious interior, deep in consultation with a group of officials. He broke off to greet them, green eyes warming into a smile.

'I'm glad you came,' he said quietly. The racing-driver's red overalls hugged his potent figure, emphasising his almost brutally male quality. He gave Lana a brief kiss on the cheek and she closed her eyes as she caught a heart-twistingly familiar whiff of expensive aftershave. Then he turned to May with that appraising smile.

'This is May Baragli,' Lana said, glad of Philip's possessive arm round her waist. 'We were at college together.'

'Baragli's a Tuscan name,' Philip said, making it a question. May looked delighted.

'That's right—my parents come from a village near Orvieto,' she nodded. The flush under her dusky skin was a direct compliment to Philip's appeal. 'Do you know Tuscany?'

'I own a few properties in the Chianti Classico region,' he smiled, making it all sound very casual. 'Two or three vineyards and some restored farmhouses I rent out.'

'Really?' May's eyes were wide as saucers.

'Tuscany's one of the most beautiful spots on earth. I go there once a year for a vacation.' He glanced at Lana. 'You must bring May to stay with us this year.' *Us?* Lana could only blink at that remark. But Philip was moving on easily. 'This is Roger Preece. He prepares my cars.'

'Nice to meet you.' Preece was a fair man in a light-coloured suit and raincoat.

'I'm afraid I have to get down to the pits right away,' Philip informed them. 'Would you like to see the car?'

Lana nodded. 'Is the rain going to make it more dangerous?' she demanded, searching his tanned face.

'It'll just make it slower,' he assured her with a grin. 'Now stop nagging!'

'Excuse me, Mr Casson.' Three or four other officials had arrived, all competing for Philip's attention. Lana and May followed at a discreet distance.

'You like him?' Lana asked, glancing at May's round face.

'Are you kidding?' May's expression was rapturous. 'Oh, what a man! That kind of charm really melts me, you know that? And that body! Six feet of hard, throbbing muscle. And the way he smiles . . .'

'You do like him,' Lana smiled.

'I simply adore him.' May shook her head. 'Of course, he's a hundred miles out of our league.'

'Why do you say that?' Lana enquired.

'It's obvious,' May shrugged. 'A man like that doesn't go out with the likes of us.'

'Why not?' Lips compressed, Lana stopped at the barrier to the pits and turned to stare at May with anxious green eyes.

'Well—he's a fabulously good-looking man, probably in his mid-thirties, and obviously richer than Rockefeller. A few properties in Tuscany! Why, he's talking about millions! He could have his pick, Lana. What are we to him? Little girls, that's what.'

'You really think so?' Lana asked, thinking wryly that if May only knew what had happened between her and Philip last night, she might change her opinions drastically!

May gave her a meaningful look. 'I *know* so. Still, it's nice to dream, isn't it? Come on.'

In the oily confusion of the pits, Lana stood staring at the crouching crimson Jaguar with the London Corporate logo emblazoned across its long bonnet and sleek sides. A mechanic was revving up the engine, making a sound unlike anything she'd ever heard from a car before.

It was like the howl of some great beast, something tearing at a chain to be free. Her heart quailed at the unearthly sound, magnified by the concrete walls, booming all around her like some primaeval warning.

Suddenly it was all horribly real to her. And far, far bigger and more alarming than she'd imagined. Philip, now anonymous in a full-face helmet, was actually going to climb into that thing and pilot it, as Roger Preece was telling them, for fifty-three laps around the twisting New York circuit. Competing with two dozen others at speeds of up to two-hundred miles an hour.

'God,' May said in awe. 'Isn't this something?'

'Yes,' Lana gritted. 'It's ridiculous male nonsense.'

'Eh?'

Shaken by the force of her own reaction, Lana turned away, hugging herself. She was wishing she hadn't come now. Today wasn't going to be fun at all. It was going to be a frightening ordeal for her. May peered into the Jaguar's cockpit, then came back to Lana, wide-eyed.

'There's only one seat in there,' she reported.

'The rest is all bare metal! And there's a huge fire-extinguisher——'

'I don't want to know,' Lana cut her off tersely. 'I wish I hadn't come!'

'He's going to be all right,' May assured her, her eyes sympathetic with understanding. 'He's done this kind of thing before, Lana.'

'What the hell does he *need* to do it for?' She clenched her teeth, staring at Philip's unheeding back. 'He's got everything he could possibly want! Why does he have to go and risk his neck in this kind of madness?'

'Maybe precisely because he's got everything,' May smiled. 'Listen, it won't help him to see you looking like that. They're just about to go to the starting grid.'

It was true. She barely had time to take in the hard squeeze from Philip's gauntleted hand, and then he was climbing into the car, being strapped in, and driving slowly out on to the glistening-wet track to join the streams of other cars.

Dry-mouthed, she had to force herself to stay calm, suppressing her impulse to turn and run.

May slipped her arm through Lana's comfortingly. 'Take it easy.'

'Not exactly your everyday sort of bank-manager, is he?' Roger Preece grinned, joining them.

'No,' Lana agreed tersely. The pick-up truck waiting in the pits with its engine running was a horribly ominous sign. It was equipped with flashing lights, and had the words EMERGENCY FIRE SERVICE painted on its orange bonnet.

They trooped up the concrete stairway to the seats that had been reserved for them above the pits, where a small group was already sitting, some watching the cars through binoculars.

Lana had already somewhat drily noted the presence of two very pretty young women, dressed in tight jeans and clingy T-shirts despite the weather. They were making very busy with clipboards and stopwatches, and had been favouring Philip with adoring glances and wiggles before the start.

'Those must be some of the fringe benefits,' May commented with a horsy grin. Lana only winced.

'Know anything about cars?' Roger Preece asked on the way up.

'Not much,' May smiled.

'It's a turbocharged vee-twelve,' Roger Preece supplied proudly. 'Triple-choke downdraught Webers, front independent suspension——'

'Is it safe?' Lana cut tensely through the incomprehensible jargon.

'If it isn't, we'll soon find out,' Preece chuckled. 'Philip usually reaches the limits it was designed for.' Oblivious to the filthy look Lana gave him, he pulled a hip-flask out of the pocket of his coat, and offered it to them. 'Something to keep out the cold.'

She took it numbly, and gulped a mouthful, choking slightly as the raw spirit burned her throat.

'They're off!'

The noise of the crowd swelled suddenly into a roar as the crowded pack of cars came flying down the straight towards them.

'That's Philip,' Roger Preece yelled, 'right in front!'

Lana was just in time to see a low-slung scarlet shape hurtle past the grandstand and swing into

the bend beyond, cornering at the very limit of the
track, the rest of the cars close at its heels.

Her heart jolted painfully. This was going to be
even worse than she'd expected. She leaned back
in her seat, the damp wind tugging golden strands
of hair loose from her carefully-prepared chignon,
praying as she'd never prayed before.

'He's made a brilliant start.' Preece had to
shout to make himself heard over the noise of
the engines and the public-address, even though
the cars were already at the other side of the
track.

'God, this is exciting,' May said, eyes bright.
'Look at them go!'

Appalled, Lana watched the field as it swept
along the far side of the track then round the bank
towards them again. The cars were beginning to
separate out now, but the red Jaguar was still
ahead, a glittering cloud of spray hanging at its
heels. As the car flashed by with a deafening howl,
she had an impression of gloved hands at the
wheel, a helmeted head behind the tinted glass.

'Exciting?' she echoed, shaking her head. 'I'm
glad you think so.'

She knew she was going to be in agony until this
race was over. Philip in that howling beast! What
the hell was he doing, trying to get himself killed?
She sat hugging herself, hardly daring to watch as
the cars screamed around the gleaming-wet track,
flicking through the bends and jockeying for
position with terrifying aggression.

'He's going so fast,' she moaned. Though he'd
increased his lead, she knew Philip was taking
frightening chances with the wet and the dangerous
curves. At each corner she felt her heart rise into
her throat for him, bringing a horrible foreboding

that he'd be killed, right here, in front of her eyes.
'God, how terrible it must be to be married to a
racing-driver!'

'I'm beginning to see what you mean,' May said,
her expression more serious now.

Lana couldn't tear her eyes away from the
snarling red missile for a single moment, as though
it contained all her hopes, all her dreams for the
future. Not even when it seemed certain he was
going to slide off the circuit into the stands could
she look away.

'Damn you,' she whispered. A mixture of terror
and fury was battling inside her; terror that he'd
crash, fury at him for risking his magnificent,
precious self in this crazy way.

The laps turned into a blur as she sat, tense and
fearful, waiting for the end. Half-an-hour into the
race, Roger Preece began to look worried. 'Pirotti
keeps trying to overtake,' he commented, the
binoculars pressed to his eyes. 'But he hasn't got
the speed. He's a bloody madman!'

The pack thundered into the straight, more
strung out now; now Lana could see a blue-and-
white car on Philip's outside, trying to force
through the gap.

'He's so close,' May said breathlessly. As they
entered the final bend into the banking, faster than
on any previous lap, the two cars seemed to touch
wheels.

Lana found herself on her feet, thrusting her
knuckles into her mouth to choke back her scream
of horror.

The blue-and-white car was reining back, white
smoke pouring from its brakes. But she only had
eyes for the Jaguar. The red car had broken into a
four-wheel drift, sliding sideways up the glistening

concrete at something over a hundred and fifty miles an hour.

And then, with disbelief, she saw the front wheel explode into a spray of black rubber fragments.

'My God!'

Everything was suddenly moving into slow-motion inside her head, like a film running down. The Jaguar was rolling over and over and over, glass and panels flying off in a shower of debris.

Over and over and over. Until it slid into the straw bales along the banking, on its crumpled roof, both doors hanging open.

And erupted into an orange fireball bright enough to hurt the eyes.

CHAPTER FIVE

'No!' Mindless with the horror of what she was seeing, Lana clawed her way past May, and stumbled down the concrete stairs, trying to get to the blazing wreckage. Her one thought was to get Philip out of there, pull him out with her bare hands if necessary——

'Hey!' Someone tried to pull her back, and she wrestled madly against the restraining hands. 'You can't do anything, Lana!' It was Roger Preece, white-faced, struggling to hold her still.

'*Let me go,*' she snarled, panic giving her a wild strength. 'I've got to go to him!'

'Don't look, Lana!' May was at her side now, clinging to her other arm, holding her back. 'Don't look at it!' There were screams and shouts among the roar of the crowd, and above it all, the

ululating note of an ambulance. Shivering, Lana
turned in agony. Silver-suited firemen were hosing
the car with white foam, and the car was
surrounded by the rescue team. Then they were
pulling Philip out of the wreckage, his tall figure
recognisable as he emerged, despite the now-
charred overalls and helmet.

'He's moving,' someone said in an awed voice.
'Look, he's alive.'

Tears of sheer, disbelieving relief were sliding
down Lana's cheeks as she saw him stumble
upright, shaking his head dazedly as they helped
him into the ambulance.

'Oh thank God,' she said in a drained voice, and
sank back into the seat, crying helplessly. It had all
happened in seconds, but had changed her world
for ever. May hugged her anxiously as she buried
her face in her hands, her whole body wracked
with delayed shock.

'He's all right,' May was saying, as though she
were gentling a frightened child. 'He's all right,
Lana.'

'How could he?' Lana looked up at May, her
pale face streaked with tears. 'How could he do
that to me?' she whispered.

'Mr Casson was lucky enough to escape with
minor injuries,' the orderly was repeating for the
tenth time for the benefit of the clustering
pressmen. 'His protective clothing shielded him
from the worst of the heat. Yes, the doctors will be
finished with him in a short while.'

'He's doing fine,' May said in a quiet voice,
squeezing Lana's arm. 'It's all over now. You'll see
him in a few moments.'

Lana nodded, unable to speak. She was still

shaking like a leaf, her nails cutting painfully into her palms. The past hour had been ghastly, with the shadow of death seemingly everywhere.

Somehow, she'd known it was going to happen. Right from the start of this day, she'd known.

She couldn't get the images out of her mind. The Jaguar engulfed by that evil scarlet orchid of flame. Her unreasoning panic, the deep sense of betrayal that had come from deep in her mind. Betrayal in that he'd made her care for him, and then had irresponsibly risked his own life.

'I don't ever want to see another one like that,' Roger Preece said tightly, as though re-living the same memories.

Lana closed her eyes, leaned back against the hospital corridor wall, and took a shuddering breath. She hadn't known just how much she cared about Philip until that moment. She hadn't known. There had been nothing like this feeling since the day her mother died, and she'd stood crying at the misty graveside, so desolate and alone . . .

'Are you all right?' May asked anxiously. Lana nodded, her voice husky.

'I'll be fine.'

She'd had plenty of time since the accident to see the future. To see the kind of life she'd have as Philip's wife, going through this private hell each time he took to the racing circuits.

'The doctors have finished.' The doors opened, and there was a stampede of pressmen towards the private ward.

'Hang on.' Roger stopped Lana's instinctive movement forward with a hand on her arm. 'Let the vultures get their business over first.'

They followed in the wake of the press. Philip

propped up in bed, naked to the waist. One shoulder was strapped, and there was a scattering of bandages, stark against his tanned skin. Lana's heart contracted at the weariness in his face, but he obviously had the strength to face the torrent of questions and the blaze of flashbulbs.

The group clustered around him, talking in excited voices. She waited, the pain in her stomach slowly easing, her sea-green eyes still blurry with the tension she'd been through.

After a few minutes, the doctors herded the reluctant pressmen out. As the room cleared, Philip's eyes met Lana's. He held his hand out to her, and she went to him with a sob.

'Philip . . .' She couldn't help closing her eyes in ecstasy as he pulled her close, kissing her mouth roughly. She could smell motor-oil on him, the animal tang of his sweat, and beneath that, the acrid smell of burning.

'I thought you were dead,' she said in a shaking voice. 'You're a bloody madman. I hate you!' But her fingers were knotting in his damp hair, her lips hungry against his mouth, his cheeks, his eyes. 'Were you trying to frighten me to death?'

'You feel marvellous,' he said huskily, crushing her to him. 'Hello, Roger. Sorry about the car.'

'Never mind the damned car,' Roger said cheerfully. 'Are you all in one piece?'

'Just a few bruises and sprains. Hello May. Did I give you all a fright?'

'You didn't have to take chances like that,' Lana said, cradled in the crook of his arm, her cheek against his bare chest.

'It wasn't his fault,' Roger said, sitting next to May at the bedside. 'It was that idiot Pirotti. He got off scot-free, too.'

'He ought to be banned for life,' May said feelingly.

'It's just racing,' Philip said indifferently. His hand was stroking Lana's golden hair. 'Next time it might be him spinning out.'

'I damn well hope it is,' Roger said vindictively. 'He deserves it.'

'Is there any chance of salvaging the Jag?' Philip asked, still holding Lana close.

'None whatsoever,' Roger said flatly. 'It's a write-off.'

Philip leaned his head back with a sigh. 'Damn. That means preparing the second car in time for Indianapolis. Think we can do it?'

'Yes, with plenty of time to spare. You're still in contention, Phil. You've only slipped down one position.'

'But I have to make it first or second at Indianapolis,' he sighed.

'You must be mad.' Now truly angry, Lana elbowed her way out of his embrace, and wiped the tears off her cheeks. He wasn't worth her tears, damn him! She'd been crying her eyes out for him, and all he could think of was the next race! 'You're all mad,' she accused.

'I'll second that,' Roger smiled.

'I'm serious,' she repeated shakily. She fought for control of her shattered emotions as she turned to Philip. 'You were almost killed out there just now—and the first thing you can think of is getting another car to go and do it all again!'

'Take it easy,' Philip said gently, reaching out to touch her cheek. She evaded his hand, her eyes blazing at him.

'It's beyond a joke, Phil. Do you know what I went through out there today?'

'I know,' he said gently, eyes tender. 'But I'm all right now.'

'You can't keep on racing after this,' she said flatly. 'For God's sake, you've got to call it a day now.'

'You mean retire from motor-racing?' He smiled. 'Right here and now? I can't do that, Lana.'

'Well I can't stand it,' she told him with trembling coldness, sitting up. She meant it. She could never go through that again, never. 'How many times do you think you can get away with it? How long do you expect people who love you to sit through that kind of ordeal?'

'Now hold on,' Roger Preece began, but Lana turned on him with a grim expression. 'You keep out of this,' she snapped, silencing him.

Philip looked at her, his expression serious. 'I can't just stop racing, Lana,' he repeated quietly. 'It's half-way through the season, and despite today, I'm well up in the points.'

'The *points*?' Disbelief made her gape for a moment. 'What is it, some kind of game?'

'It's precisely because it isn't a game that I can't quit,' he said gently. 'There are tens of thousands of dollars invested in this, Lana. Almost fifty thousand in the cars alone. Thousands of hours of precious time. The interests of all sorts of people, including the other sponsors who pay to have their names on the Jaguar.' He met her rebellious eyes. 'The only way I can recoup all that investment is to finish the season high up in the points, preferably in the first three. The amount of exposure that will give London Corporate will more than repay what we've put into it. If I quit now, all that money will go to waste.'

'Money!' Lana spat, her recent anguish making her anger all the more fierce. 'How many thousands is your life worth, Philip?'

'Crashes are comparatively rare,' he said mildly.

'You don't have to have more than one to get killed,' she pointed out bitterly.

Roger Preece leaned forward. 'Lana,' he said gently, 'we all know how you feel. But Philip Casson is something unique. The racing banker— he's a phenomenon. The publicity involved is incalculable. You must see that what you're asking is impossible.'

'Aren't you already a multi-millionaire?' May said, coming down on Lana's side. 'You don't really *need* the extra business, Mr Casson, surely?'

'I have plenty of business in Europe,' he nodded. He sat up, wincing. 'But here in America I'm a comparative newcomer. Within a few months I'll be opening a new branch in New York, and I need all the media coverage I can get. The Touring Car Championship will give me everything I need.'

'But haven't you already caused enough of a sensation?' Lana demanded desperately, seeing that billowing fireball in her mind again.

'In racing,' he smiled tiredly, 'only the winners get noticed.' He took her hand, speaking only to her. 'Listen to me, Lana. I started racing five years ago. Just entering in one or two races at a time— getting my toes wet, so to speak. The year before last, I did the full circuit for the first time. I came eleventh. Last year I invested a lot more time and money, and hired Roger here to look after my cars. That time we came seventh.'

'Only because of bad luck,' Roger put in.

'This year,' Philip went on, his eyes holding

Lana's, 'I can finish in the first three, I know it. That'll mean a blaze of publicity for the Bank. The kind of launch every new business dreams of. Millions of dollars' worth of new business. And then, I promise you, I'll think about giving up racing for good. But there are still six races to go this year——'

'Six races?' she said in horror. 'Do you think I can go through today six more times?'

Philip glanced at Roger. 'Will you excuse us for a moment, Roger?'

'Of course.' Roger Preece rose, and led May outside, leaving Lana alone with Philip. She was still shaking, trying to keep her passion under control.

'You must realise by now that I care about you,' he said without preamble, his voice harsh. 'I know you care about me. But this isn't something I can just give up.' His eyes probed hers intently. 'I need your support, Lana. Not your opposition.'

'I can't live with it,' she said, pale-faced. She was feeling a cold despair blowing through her like a merciless wind. 'I realised that today. Long before the accident, Philip. I simply can't afford to let myself get involved with someone who might— might be killed any weekend in a racing-car.'

'You're not the first woman in the world to say those words,' he said with a hint of dryness. 'Fear is an occupational hazard of loving a racing driver. Some women can live with it. Others can't. You have to make up your own mind.'

'But you aren't a professional,' she pointed out unsteadily. 'You don't *need* to do this! It's just a hobby!'

'It may have been once. But it's a lot more than a hobby now. Even if I wanted to pull out,' he said impatiently, '—and believe me, days like today make me want to do just that—I couldn't. I've got to do it now.'

'Well you can do it without me,' she snapped at him defiantly.

'That's not something you can say lightly,' Philip said in a quiet voice. His body was motionless, his face as though carved from granite.

'I'm not saying it lightly.' She could hardly believe the words they were both saying, and yet she knew she meant them.

'Can you really tell me you care that little?' he asked gently.

'Of course I care,' she retorted, turning to him furiously. How could he be so obtuse? 'Listen, Phil, I lost my mother when I was thirteen years old. I know what it feels like. And I'm not going through that again, just because you want to play the hero!'

'I'm not trying to play the hero, Lana.'

'Then you're doing it for the money, which is worse!' She was realising bitterly that if last night had ended the way she'd really wanted it to, it would be impossible to say what she was saying now.

'Lana,' Philip said urgently, taking her hands, 'I could retire from motor-racing and be knocked down by a bus tomorrow. So could you, God forbid, and if that's what fate has planned for us, there's no way we can escape it. But if we all refused to get involved because we might lose our partners, there wouldn't be any more marriages or children or lovers in the world!'

'Don't treat me as though I were an idiot,' Lana retorted, brittle with nerves. 'Of course we all have to die someday. That doesn't mean we have to deliberately try and kill ourselves.' She pulled her hands away, smudged with burned oil from Philip's body. 'It's just a playboy's hobby, Phil! You can't justify risking your life like this, not for anything, let alone some kind of—of ego-trip!'

'Very well,' he said tonelessly. 'Then you'd better stay out of my life. There isn't a place for doom-ridden females in racing, Lana. They're bad luck.'

There was a taut silence. It had reached a point, she knew, where she either had to back down or give in. There was no middle way. She rose, aching inside, but fuelled by her anger against him.

'I'd better go, then, hadn't I?' Her voice rasped in her throat. She had a sudden bleak vision of the rest of her life, empty and sterile. Of herself, caught forever in a love for a dead man.

Get out now, her mind told her. *Now, while the going's good.*

She tore her eyes away from his, and walked to the door.

'Lana!'

She stopped but didn't turn round, not wanting him to see the tears on her face. 'I'll speak to you later,' he said, his voice husky with tiredness. 'At your apartment. All right?'

'What's there to talk about?' she challenged in a choked voice, knowing that if she looked at him again she'd be lost. She pushed blindly through the door.

'Come on,' she told May, with a brittle smile, 'we're going.'

'What about Philip?' May protested in surprise, but Lana was already half-way down the corridor.

CHAPTER SIX

THE doorbell dragged her from the depths of a deep, almost drugged sleep. It was hours since she'd got back from the race-track, and the apartment was dark as she walked dazedly to answer the door, knotting her gown with numbed fingers.

It was Philip.

'Oh,' Lana gasped, pushing her tumbled hair away from her face and noticing that his arm was in a loose sling. 'Are—are you all right, Phil?'

'Apart from a few aches, I'm fine,' he nodded. He didn't kiss her, and she didn't offer herself to be kissed. His face was tired, as though he hadn't had much rest after the accident. 'I came to see how you were.'

'I—I was just lying down.' Her heart thudding heavily, she let him in, switching on a table-lamp to provide a soft light. She slumped back into the sofa, feeling like a rag doll. How in God's name was she going to deal with this? She wasn't ready for the emotions waiting inside her, didn't want to face them yet. 'Make yourself a drink if you want,' she invited.

He shook his head. 'Alcohol doesn't go with painkillers.' Deep green eyes probed hers. 'Have you recovered from your little outburst of this morning, Lana?'

She closed her eyes, living through the agony of that morning again. Pain awoke in her, but it brought with it a kind of strength to say what had to be said. 'It wasn't an outburst,' she said in a low voice, clinging to her own arms, as if to protect herself from him. 'I meant every word of what I said then.'

'I see.' Harsh lines had appeared around his mouth. 'I hoped you'd have recognised by now that you were slightly hysterical as a result of the shock.'

'Hysteria?' She shook her head, wondering that he could understand her so little. 'It was the result of cold logic, Philip. Oh yes, maybe I was emotional and shaken. So would you have been if you'd been torn up inside the way I was. But my mind was working perfectly clearly. And it's working clearly now!' She was shivering now, and he came to sit beside her, his expression intent.

'I'm sorry, Lana,' he said quietly. 'I'm sorry you had to see that accident. I'd give anything for you not to have seen it. But I climbed out of it, my love. I'm here now.'

'How many times do you think you can keep climbing out?' she asked, her voice catching in her throat. 'There's a little granite monument at that track, Philip. Have you ever seen it?'

'Yes,' he said grimly.

'All the names of the drivers who've died there are carved on it,' she went on in the same bitter voice. 'I had plenty of time to read them all while I waited to find out whether you were going to live or die.' Emotion broke through her self-control, and she dug her fingers into his arm. 'For God's sake, try and put yourself in my place! How would you feel if I asked you to watch me playing with my life? Could you live with that?'

'Let's not argue,' he said, shaking his head with a touch of impatience. 'I came here to suggest a compromise. Let me finish this season—six more races—and I'll think about giving it up for good.'

'Six more races,' she repeated turning her face away. There was a sour taste in her mouth, an ache inside her that felt like bleeding. 'There speaks the rational banker! The only bargain you can make with me is to give up this insane hobby of yours here and now.'

'You know that it isn't a hobby,' he said quietly. 'And you know that I can't give it up.'

'Then you'd better give permanent relationships up instead,' she snapped, still not looking at him.

'Perhaps I should,' he said grimly. He reached for her shoulder, pulling her round to face his angry eyes. 'I thought you'd be with me on this, Lana, not fighting me, not now.'

'Oh,' she sneered, her mouth twisting, 'you want me to join the queue of Philip Casson fans? Become one of those simpering creatures in tight jeans, with a clipboard and a stopwatch? No chance, Philip! I have more self-respect than that.'

'Self-respect!' he rasped, dark brows descending. 'That's all you seem to care about.'

'Well if I'm so shallow, you're better off without me, aren't you?' she retorted, close to tears.

'Lana,' he said wearily, 'I thought you were beginning to care about me.'

'Oh, I was,' she said with biting irony. 'I'll come to your funeral.'

'That's not like you,' he said quietly.

Her eyes filled with tears, making them swim. 'Oh, Phil, I'm sorry. I just don't understand how you can keep climbing into that car, knowing that you're going to be killed in it one day.'

'I presume you expect to die in bed?' he enquired, raising an eyebrow. 'Yet that doesn't stop you from getting into bed every night.'

'My bed doesn't travel at two hundred miles an

hour,' she said, resting her forehead on her clasped arms and closing her eyes. 'I can't stand it, Philip. I mean that. I don't——' She felt the tears rise, and fought them down. 'I don't want this relationship to—to go any further. Not now that I know what sort of life it would be for me.'

'You seem to forget that we're still linked by a business arrangement,' he said drily.

She bit her lip. Yes, their business arrangement. How ironic! And how little it seemed to matter now, in the unbearable loss of this moment.

And yet, her treacherous heart whispered, their business contact would be a way of not losing Philip altogether. A reason to keep seeing him, even though there would be nothing more between them.

An excuse.

A flame of hope flickered in her darkness now. At least that way she'd have some tiny contact with him, a lifeline to Philip that might save her from the worst misery that was threatening to engulf her.

Lana raised her head slowly. 'No, I haven't forgotten,' she said quietly. 'But I don't see what that has to do with anything.'

'You're telling me you really think you can keep our relationship on a business level?' he enquired, lifting one eyebrow in disbelief.

'That's exactly what I'm telling you,' she nodded, trying to sound as though she really meant the cool words. 'After all, that's what we started out with. It was only last night—last night that we——' She faltered on the words, tearing her eyes away from his level gaze. Dear God, let him not hate her for sounding so callous! 'I want to—to forget that anything happened between us, Philip. Anything emotional, I mean. Let's just keep it on a business level from now on, and do what we have to do without hurting each other any more.'

'You little——' He didn't say the word, but his voice cut like a lash for all its velvet. 'A business level, eh?' His mouth a hard, bitter line, he rose to his full height, looking down at her with an expression that made her flinch. 'And you have the gall to preach to me about my lack of feeling?'

She'd asked for it, she thought miserably, lowering her eyes. 'We could at least—at least stay friends that way,' she mumbled. 'Not lose each other for ever——'

'Friends,' he repeated drily. 'We were almost lovers!'

'But we didn't become lovers,' she said. 'Maybe we should be grateful for that. It leaves us room to adapt, doesn't it?'

'What the hell are you talking about?' Philip rasped.

'I mean that if we'd—if we'd made love, and this had happened, we'd have had no choice but to leave each other.' She groped after the words hesitantly. 'This way, maybe we can salvage something out of the ashes. Friendship.' His expression was savage enough to make her wince. 'If not that, then at least mutual respect——'

'I wouldn't say any more if I were you,' he told her grimly. 'You've already made your position abundantly clear.' He rubbed his face wearily, closing his eyes. 'I've been such a damned fool, right from the start, haven't I? And I don't have any excuse. Something drew me to you, Lana, so strongly that I forgot the most elementary rules of caution. You weren't ready for love, and I was pushing far, far too hard.'

'Oh Phil——' she said unhappily.

For a moment she thought he was going to say more, but his face was closed, unyielding as granite. 'Please don't expect me to slip into the role of your sexless friend, Lana. I'm not cut out for it.' He looked at her with hard, weary eyes. 'But for your father's sake, I'm not going to tell you to go to hell. If you want my bank to finance you, so be it. I'll be in touch when we're ready to sign the contract. Does that suit you?'

She winced at the biting tone, but gritted her teeth. 'That suits me very well,' she said evenly. But she wanted to say something, anything, to make him understand. 'Phil, you can't know how sorry I am——'

'Please let's not have any sentimental speeches,' he cut through her words. 'They wouldn't suit you. As you said, there was nothing to be sentimental over in the first place, was there? Don't get up,' he finished, his face like flint. 'I know my way out.'

When the door closed behind him, Lana rose on shaky legs, and went into the kitchen to make herself a cup of coffee. She was sick to her stomach, yet she knew she should eat something.

Had she deserved that look on his face? It didn't matter, anyway. All that mattered was that she'd freed herself from a relationship which had no future.

She sawed at the bread, wishing her hands weren't quite so weak and trembling. A business relationship. She couldn't blame herself for wanting that, at least, that slender line to Philip Casson. It was all she could afford. Her foray into the world of steamy romance had ended with unexpected swiftness and ignominy. And when Philip saw her again, she knew, it would be very hard to bear the contempt in his face. She'd better start trying to be cool towards him, but fast.

She saw his face in her mind again. The look in his eyes, hard and bitter and betrayed.

The knife tumbled out of her fingers, and she crumpled into the kitchen chair, crying as though her heart would break.

'You can't mean it,' May said in dismay over the restaurant table. 'You can't be throwing it all away because of that accident?'

'I'm not throwing anything away,' Lana said tersely. She was still shaking. 'There's nothing *to* throw away.'

'Of course there is,' May said, her eyes widening. 'You and Philip—why, I thought it was going to be the romance of the year!'

'I don't want to talk about it.' But she couldn't get Philip out of her mind. Her fear for him was sitting inside her, a ball of emotion that was stopping her from eating the Chinese meal which May had just bought her.

'You don't want to talk about it? But he's crazy about you,' May argued, looking as though she still couldn't believe that Lana was serious.

Lana's face was pale as she fiddled with her chopsticks. The shadows under her clear green eyes bore mute testimony to the quality of her sleep over the week since that terrible day at the track.

'Not that crazy,' she said tersely.

'Couldn't you persuade him——?' May didn't finish the futile question as Lana shook her head. In her mind's eye, that ball of flame was exploding around the Jaguar again, searing and blistering the brave scarlet paint.

'He can't care what other people feel,' Lana said jerkily. 'How can I love someone like that?'

May slipped a comforting arm round her shoulders.

'He does care,' she said gently. 'But he's his own man. You can't expect to change him with a few tears.' She smiled ruefully. 'I've never seen you so depressed. You've got to do something to shake yourself out of this, Lana.'

'I'm going to,' Lana said with an effort. 'Lionel Webber's taking me out for the day on Saturday.'

'You mean Mister Millions?' May grinned. Lionel Webber Junior, blue-eyed and blond, handsome, athletic, and just twenty-five, was the heir presumptive to the Webber oil empire. And also, of course, one of the primest two-hundredweights' worth of marriageable beef on the market. 'He ought to provide a welcome distraction!'

'Yes,' Lana said tiredly. 'He's pushy, that's all.'

'He could push *me* anywhere,' May sighed. Lana felt a pang of wry amusement. Compared to Philip, Lionel Webber was little more than a brash boy who'd had it all his own way since infancy. But she couldn't explain distinctions like that to May.

They left the restaurant and walked slowly down Pearl Street in the brilliant sunshine, taking in the exotic atmosphere of shops covered with Chinese writing, sidewalks crowded with more Eastern faces than Western ones.

They stopped at a street corner. The Chinese greengrocer's shop opposite was advertising lotus roots, winter melon and snow peas.

'Can I ask you something?' May said, slipping her arm through Lana's.

'Hmmm.'

'How serious *were* you about Philip Casson?'

Lana didn't answer. She was remembering that billowing orange flame. All that beautiful strength, that nobility, destroyed—like a child's nightmare, the picture refused to leave her, haunting her thoughts.

'Well,' May went on practically, 'if anything, what you're going through now proves that you were right not to get further involved with him. Not so?'

'I suppose you're right,' Lana sighed. But there was more to it than that; she *was* involved, that was the irony. And with a sense of bruised wonder she was realising just how much she did care for Philip Casson.

After parting from May, she took the subway to Fifth Avenue, and walked slowly through the crowds, staring into the glittering windows and trying to focus on the fashion ideas on display. But her eyes were glazed, and her thoughts were constantly of Philip.

God, she was missing him! So much excitement had built up in her over him. A sense of wonder, a thrill that had gone deep into her mind.

Feeling all that hope and anticipation die in her was cruelly painful.

And the bitterest irony of all was that refusing to see him hadn't lessened her anxiety in the slightest. There had been a picture of him in the *New York Times* that morning, together with an article about the race at Indianapolis at the end of the month. Within a few weeks he was going to be racing again, stretching thin the precious filament of his life. And she was going to enter her private little hell again.

Yet there was no going back. Even if she'd wanted to recant, run to Philip and beg him to take her back, she wasn't sure he'd take her now. She'd done too much damage to their budding relationship. Things killed at the growing stage just didn't come alive again.

When Lionel Webber had called, inviting her to partner him at tennis that Saturday, she'd jumped at the invitation with an eagerness which must have quite flattered him. She'd have welcomed any kind of distraction from her own thoughts, and even though Lionel sometimes irritated her to death, at least he had enough force of personality to make her forget about Philip for a day, at least.

CHAPTER SEVEN

On Saturday, however, she was beginning to doubt whether the remedy was worth the cure. She'd forgotten all the things she resented about Lionel—one of them being the way he automatically assumed it was a male prerogative to drive her car.

He'd arrived to pick her up in an exquisite Mercedes sports convertible, a far more feminine car than her own. It had been a gift from Lionel J. Webber Snr to his eldest son.

'We're going in your car,' he informed her with a glint in his eye.

'But why? I like yours.'

'Yours is faster.'

The answer hadn't exactly reassured her, and
when he'd insisted on taking the keys to the
Porsche from her, she'd been even less reassured.
He'd driven the last time they'd gone out
together—fast.

'What's under that bonnet,' he grinned, 'is not
for little girls to play with.'

'Don't patronise,' she retorted acidly. 'I'm
perfectly capable of driving my own car.'

'You little beauty.' He wasn't talking to her; he
was crooning over the metallic-blue bonnet. Lana
sighed. Wealth and good looks were almost wasted
on someone like Lionel Webber. He had the
square-jawed, masculine appeal of his father, and
a lot of the push; but she'd always felt that he
hadn't quite grown up yet. He was the sort of
American male who took an intense pride in the
excellence of his tennis, his driving ability and his
supposed sexual prowess, and who never opened a
book.

He hadn't even noticed the plain cream silk
shirt-dress she was wearing. Its deliciously severe
lines were pure genius, and any fashionable
woman's head would have turned, but Lionel
hadn't even blinked.

Still, he could be amusing when he wasn't trying
to impress, and the drive out to Huntingdon was
pleasant enough to take her mind off thoughts of
Philip.

'Isn't it a lovely day?' She turned her face up to
the sun like a cat. 'I love the country.'

'Reminds you of England, huh?' He was
driving fast, but not dangerously so, and she had
to admit he was a better driver than she was.
And the New Jersey countryside was not unlike
England. It all gave her a chance to relax her

mind, and try and get out from under the clouds for a while.

She talked happily about her schooldays in Devon all the way, aware that he was probably much more interested in the car's performance than in her monologue, but not caring.

The Huntingdon Country Club, where they were going, was formidably exclusive. Only white Anglo-Saxon Protestants were welcome within its ivy-clad precincts, and the whole place had an expensive, well-laundered air. A smug air of having insulated itself successfully from the outside world.

Lana had met their tennis opponents before. Tom McNally was a successful corporate lawyer in his late twenties; his wife Sheree, much younger than Tom, had been a model for a year or two before her marriage.

'Let's go into the lounge and have a drink before lunch,' Tom suggested jovially.

As they sat down in the long, sunlit room where some of the other members were watching the Saturday afternoon sports coverage on television, Lana reflected that she didn't like either of them particularly. They were both groomed, good-looking and confident, like people out of a cigarette advertisement. They were Lionel's sort of people, not hers. Trendy New Yorkers, moneyed and smug.

What would Philip Casson make of Tom and Lionel? Maybe he'd spoiled her for lesser men—for good. Lana tried to put aside her sourness, and join in with the conversation.

She was just finishing her drink when something on the television screen in the corner caught her eye. Something she remembered all too well. Philip's scarlet Jaguar tumbling over and over, now caught in the unreal web of the slow-motion camera. She bit her lip hard as that orange ball of flame erupted around the upside-down car, blistering the bright paint, pouring black smoke into the rainy air.

The frame froze on the picture of the marshals hauling Philip out of the wreckage, then cut to a brightly-lit interview room.

'Excuse me,' she said awkwardly, rising hastily, 'there's something I want to watch.'

Oblivious to their surprise, Lana picked up her drink and hurried over to the set to hear the interview.

The camera was zooming in on Philip's tanned face, laughing at something the interviewer had said.

'Yes,' he nodded, the two-dimensional screen making his image somehow unreal. 'I'll certainly be at Indianapolis. And at Detroit, and at Las Vegas, too.'

'So no retirement?' the interviewer prompted.

A dismissive gesture. 'Not just yet. I have a few races left in me.'

'Philip Casson, you're on record as one of the most talented amateurs in the game. But isn't amateur racing an expensive hobby? Especially when people like Pirotti do what we've just seen to a twenty-thousand-dollar car?'

Again that smile. 'Alessandro Pirotti and I are good friends, Howard, and I don't blame him in the least. We can all make mistakes. But there's no question that it's frighteningly expensive. It has its compensations, though.'

'It's certainly getting the name of London Corporate known to a lot of people,' the interviewer smiled. 'As the owner-director of one of England's most successful merchant banks, I presume you pay your own bills?'

'Most of them.' He leaned back, interlacing his fingers, eyes clear green under the arc lights. 'The real costs aren't in dollars, though.'

'Are you talking about the crashes?'

'Yes, partly. Motor racing is a lonely sport, and not just because you're all alone in that cockpit. It's lonely because you become a bad risk for other people to love.' Lana felt a dull pain sink through her heart.

'A bad risk?' The interviewer was looking as though he'd scented a story. 'Phil, we've been hearing a lot recently about the pressures of motor-racing. We've seen at least two marriages break up this year, principally because the wives couldn't stand the constant anxieties of the sport.' Philip nodded. 'Are you saying that something similar has now happened to you?'

'I'm not married.' Philip's image looked into the camera, into Lana's eyes, into her soul. 'But I've lost more than I care to think about sometimes.'

'Do you want to expand on that?'

Philip smiled, erasing the moment as though it had never been. 'No.'

'Would you like to comment on the recent divorce between the ex-champion Aldo Carrera and his wife?'

'I never make comments about my friends' private lives,' Philip said dismissively.

'Let's turn to your prospects for Indianapolis, then, Philip. Who do you see as your biggest rival?'

She listened to the rest of the interview in

silence, until it ended and was replaced by an item on ice-hockey.

Disturbed, she stared vacantly into her glass. So he was feeling the pain, too. But it didn't change anything. Racing was his choice, she thought harshly. No one was forcing him into it.

The other three were looking at her curiously as she returned to the table. 'Just a friend of mine,' she explained with a stiff smile. 'I'm sorry.'

'Philip Casson's a friend of yours?' Tom queried. 'You'd better watch your laurels, Lionel.' There was laughter. They all had, Lana thought, the same impregnable self-confidence. Unlike her, none of them were haunted by unhappiness or doubt.

'He's very nice,' Sheree said speculatively, sipping her drink. 'Is he a good friend, Lana?'

'A business acquaintance,' Lana replied, not missing the slight emphasis on the word *good*.

'He was lucky to get out of that crash alive,' Sheree went on, watching Lana's face as though for a reaction. 'He could have been really badly burned. Or mutilated. Couldn't he? Fire can do terrible things to a man.'

'Yes,' Lana said tightly, feeling sickness rise in her, 'it can.' There was a sparkle in Sheree's blue eyes now as she dropped her gaze. Well done, Lana thought sourly, my expression must have told you exactly what you wanted to know.

After that it was something of an effort to drag herself around the tennis court for two doubles matches. She told herself the exercise was doing her good, though, and felt that the afternoon had served its purpose when she realised she hadn't thought of Philip for over an hour.

Mainly due to Lionel's mighty ground-strokes they won the match easily. Winning put Lionel in an even better mood, and his handsome face was glowing as he threw her a 'Well done, partner,' and they went off for their respective showers.

After an English-style cream tea in the lounge, the party broke up.

Lionel was still high with victory as they set off back to New York. Shadows were lengthening across the road, and there was little traffic. As though his confidence had been boosted, he was driving the Porsche fast now, the needle flickering constantly around the eighty mark.

'You're really sweet on that Philip Casson guy, aren't you?' he asked suddenly, grinning at her.

'I told you,' she retorted, 'he's someone I know through business, that's all.'

'Come off it. Sheree says you're crazy about him.'

'Oh?' Dislike made Lana's face freeze. 'Since when is Sheree McNally an expert on my life?'

'She says she saw you out with him a month ago, at some night-club. Dancing cheek-to-cheek. And you looked really sick after you'd watched that interview this afternoon.'

'I don't like seeing people I know risk their lives, Lionel,' she told him grimly. 'That's not unusual.'

'It's not unusual,' he hummed with a smirk, 'to be in love with anyone . . . I just love this car. Want to sell it?'

'No,' she said shortly, glad to be off the topic of Philip Casson. 'I do not want to sell it. I worked damned hard to buy it.'

'Swap it for my Merc, then?'

'Oh, Lionel, grow up. People don't swap their cars.'

'That's the trouble with you, Lana,' he sighed. 'No imagination.'

*　　*　　*

She hadn't wanted to wear anything too outrageous for her father's cocktail party, so she'd settled for one of the designs she'd knitted up and then rejected for the American Fashions collection, a black and silver dolman which made the most of her rather less than voluptuous breasts while flattering the slender line of her waist.

Sleek green silk pants and a minimum of jewellery helped maintain the quietly elegant mood, and she'd casually swept the heavy gold hair away from the nape of her neck, securing it with an old silver Mexican clasp her mother had given her long ago. The outfit made her look young, supple, light, a look she personally preferred.

She arrived in the early stages of the evening, glad that Susan Bates was on hand to do the hostessing. These days she didn't feel up to any kind of ordeal. Crowds made her shy and uncertain at the best of times, but right now, she just didn't seem to have the heart for anything.

The guests were gathering in groups around the bar on the patio and in the garden, the buzz of conversation promising a lively night ahead. Her father was at the centre of the biggest group on the lawn.

'You look lovely,' he smiled, coming over to meet her. 'I'm so glad you're here. Come along, and I'll introduce you to some people you should know.' He put his arm round her shoulders and drew her into the group. 'I'd like you all to meet my daughter Lana. I think you've met Esther Peters? This is Doktor Schultz, the German Consul, and his wife Irma . . .'

Lana nodded and smiled, murmuring hullos as

the guests were introduced and making an effort to
be pleasant. Little cocktail party indeed! The
Chinese Consul and her husband were here, as
well as the French Ambassador, on a flying visit
from Washington. Everyone here was rich,
important or talented. New York society was well
represented by the usual bright crowd of financiers,
TV and film personalities, opera singers and city
politicians.

May Baragli arrived a few minutes after eight,
looking ravishing in a red cocktail dress which set
her Italianate looks off to voluptuous perfection.
There was, as her father had promised, no
shortage of young men eager to talk and flirt, and
the party gradually separated into two groups, the
younger and noisier of which congregated at the
bar.

May was steadfastly cheerful, studiously avoiding any mention of Philip—for which Lana was
grateful. Lana enthused over her dress.

'Yes,' May sighed in answer to Lana's question
as to whether she'd made it herself. 'I really had
fun dreaming it up. My efforts for Rosenberg's
pay well enough, but there's no glamour in it.
Know what I've been doing all week? Designing a
range of sensible maternity wear in polyester
cotton mixes. *Sensible*. I ask you.'

Lana smiled at May's expression. '*Haute
couture* can be just as boring, I assure you.'

'I guess you've got a flair for fashion and I
haven't,' May admitted, 'and that's that.' May
sipped her drink. 'Nice party. You Brits really
know how to lay things on.' The evening was in
full swing. The lanterns had come on now that the
sun was down, and a magical light made
everything beautiful. She heard her father's bark

of laughter across the lawn. He had little idea of how her relationship with Philip Casson had turned out. Sooner or later she'd have to give him some idea of what had happened—at least to avoid any potentially embarrassing situations arising.

People found her father so charming, and not just because it was his job to be charming. But he'd been lonely since her mother's death. He'd never remarried. A senior diplomat without a wife was something of a rarity these days, but Wetherby Fox's ability was such that his career had simply kept on blossoming. Very few people knew of the secret grief he always carried inside.

Suddenly she stopped in shock. Philip! She hadn't seen him arrive, but he was now standing with her father, smiling as they both listened to the German Consul.

Lana's heart froze for a second. What had she just been thinking about awkward situations arising? She tried hastily to efface herself behind a palm, but at that moment her father caught sight of her.

'Lana!' he called, 'come and join us.'

She had little choice but to trudge unwillingly over to the small group. The Consul-General was smiling happily, oblivious to his daughter's unhappy expression.

'Hello, Lana.' Philip held out his hand, eyes glinting. She gave him a set of nerveless fingers, avoiding his eyes.

'Hello, Philip,' she said levelly, trying not to show him how much seeing him had upset her. The white evening-jacket suited him to perfection; despite the grey streaks in his thick, dark hair, he might have seemed young to have achieved so much, were it not for the natural authority that he commanded. Seeing him was like a hand grasping her heart, squeezing it tight.

Philip's eyes drifted down her figure, crude as a wolf-whistle. He smiled lazily. 'Well, well. You belong on the front cover of *Vogue*. Is that top your own design?'

She nodded bleakly.

'She's her own best advertisement,' her father put in cheerfully. The other members of the group, watching Lana indulgently, murmured assent.

'I hear that London Corporate are going to back you in a new venture,' Dr Schultz said innocently to Lana. 'You are very lucky.'

Lana tried to retrieve some of her poise. 'Yes, I am,' she nodded, and left it at that.

Wetherby Fox glanced at his daughter's expression, puzzled. 'All right?' he murmured.

'Never better,' she gritted.

'Good. Lana's getting out of touch with England,' he told Philip confidentially. 'She only meets Americans these days. See if you can rub a bit of English culture off on her.'

'I'll do my best,' Philip said gravely.

Lana cursed her father's well-meant humour. 'Excuse me,' she said, deciding it would be as well to leave right now, 'I want to talk to May——'

'Oh, you can see her every day,' her father smiled. 'Stay and look after Philip. After all, he is going to make your fortune, isn't he?'

'I am indeed,' Philip said urbanely. He took Lana's arm with all the familiarity of a lover, and led her away from the group. 'Smile,' he commanded with amusement. 'You're supposed to be playing the genial hostess, my dear Lana.'

She pulled her arm firmly away from his. 'You

don't have to get so close, Philip,' she said in a low voice. 'I thought we didn't have anything to say to each other. Why are you here?'

'Because your father invited me weeks ago,' he replied. 'Besides, I wanted to see how you were.' Completely at his ease, he brushed a tendril of her blonde hair away from her forehead. She flinched at the intimacy. 'You promised to take good care of me. Why not show me round the pretty flowers?'

'After what I said to you last time we met,' she said through clenched teeth, 'it might have been more sensible of you to avoid meeting me socially. It can only upset both of us!'

'I'm not upset,' he contradicted her with a wicked glint in his green eyes. 'Are you?'

'I——' She broke off, not knowing what to say.

'If you want to pretend that nothing has ever happened between us,' he went on, 'then you're sticking your head in the sand.'

'Nothing *has* happened between us,' she threw at him, trying to sound as though she meant it. 'You're just lending me money. That's all.'

'That's all? He was still lazily appreciating her figure, his eyes seeming to take the slender lines of her body apart, muscle by muscle.

'Stop *looking* at me like that,' she commanded waspishly. 'It's an insult!'

'Really?' he drawled. 'Some women would call it a compliment.'

'To be mentally undressed by you?' she retorted.

'Oh, I undressed you from across the lawn,' he said calmly. 'I'm a long way past that stage now.' The heavy-lidded eyes made her heart turn, as though electrodes had been pushed into her stomach.

'I don't have to take this,' she said, turning to

leave. Iron fingers bit into her arm, pulling her round to face him again. The amusement in his face had given way to anger now.

'Stop behaving like a schoolgirl,' he rasped. 'Do you really think that we're over, just because you say so?'

'We're over because of your total inability to respect my feelings,' she said fiercely. 'Because you just don't give a damn what anyone else feels.'

'You know that's rubbish,' he said impatiently, still holding her arm tightly. 'I wouldn't even be here, making a fool of myself, if I didn't care about you!'

People were beginning to glance at them now, and Lana felt humiliation colour her cheeks.

'Let me go,' she commanded. 'People are looking.'

'Then let's go somewhere they won't watch,' he said.

Lana hesitated; then, feeling speculative eyes on them, led him through the rose-garden to the swimming-pool, which was shimmering turquoise in the evening light.

'You didn't have to make a scene,' she accused shakily.

'Listen to me, Lana,' he said, more gently, 'I know you had a frightening, upsetting experience that day. You shouldn't have had to go through it, and I'm deeply sorry you did. But you have to understand how important the championship is to me.'

'It's not more important than your life,' she flared at him. The ache returned, and she felt the hard lump forming in her throat. 'Oh, hell. We've been through all this already, Phil. There just isn't anything more to add.'

They were in the heavily-scented shade of a magnolia tree at the poolside, and he reached out to pluck one of the creamy blossoms. He held it to his nose, inhaling its perfume.

'Well, well.' He was watching her over the flower, his lean face almost amused. 'You must be tougher than I imagined.'

'Or perhaps your famous charm is less potent than you imagined?' she suggested sharply. He made her tremble inside, partly from anger, partly from some other emotion that she didn't want to name, yet she was damned if she'd let him see that. Who the hell did he think he was, anyway? 'I've already made it perfectly clear that I see no future in our relationship so long as you keep racing,' she went on coldly. 'I can't afford to allow myself to be involved with a man who risks his life for a ridiculous contest.'

'Afford? Allow?' He shook his head. 'You talk like some kind of computer. Our emotions aren't that easily controlled, Lana. We're not computers.'

'You're the expert,' she shrugged sullenly. 'You ought to know.'

'I do know,' he nodded. 'I know that you care about me, every bit as much as I care about you.'

'Really?' Fighting down the emotion his words had stirred in her, she clenched her hands behind her back. 'I think you're wrong, Philip. I can control my feelings. And in this case, I fully intend to! And if you want to withdraw from the deal we were planning, please do so. I can always find backing somewhere else.'

'I have no intention of withdrawing from our deal,' he said calmly.

'Nor do I,' she said grimly.

'Bravo.' He leaned forward and presented her

with the magnolia blossom. 'Sweets to the sweet.'
A burst of laughter from the party floated to them
on the still evening air, offering her a chance of
escape.

'Excuse me, Philip. I have to get back to the
party.'

'The party's doing fine without you,' he pointed
out gently. She flinched as he reached out to
stroke her cheek. 'According to your father,' he
said smoothly, 'I'm supposed to be rubbing
something off on you. Now what was it?'

'I think you must get some kind of twisted
pleasure out of tormenting me,' she said sourly.

'What a horrible little girl you are,' he said,
eyebrows soaring.

'Oh, don't play the innocent,' she accused in
exasperation. 'You do it deliberately.'

'And you're quite delicious,' he murmured,
tracing the delicate shape of her mouth with his
fingertips. 'Even when you're being perfectly foul.
Did you know that?'

'I must go—I mean it!' Lana hissed, mesmerised
by his caress.

'So do I.' He drew her close, his mouth coming
down on hers with warm lips. His smell was
dizzying, reminding her unbearably of past times
when they'd touched like this. She wanted
desperately to struggle, but he paralysed her
somehow, as though his gentleness were the most
brutal force. He kissed her almost as he might
have kissed a child, holding her against his lean
body so that she could feel the hardness of his
muscles under the silk.

'Why, you're shaking,' he said softly, the husky
laughter not far underneath his words. 'You're
supposed to be totally indifferent to me. Aren't you?'

'Let me go now.' He made her senses swim. She put her palms on his chest to push him away, and made an effort to control the wavering in her voice. 'You've had your little game, Phil——'

'It's no game,' he growled. 'The sooner you realise that, the better!' He kissed her again, with almost savage desire now, bruising her lips against her teeth, making her whimper with pain.

Her arrogance seemed to deflate like a punctured balloon. 'Philip,' she whispered against his cheek, bitter hurt making her want to curl up and die. 'Oh, Philip, I need you so much . . .'

'Exactly.' He held her with deep tenderness, his lips warm against her temple. 'Just as I need you, my love.' His voice was a husky murmur, melting her from within. 'Neither of us wants to do without the other. Let's talk this whole thing through, hmmm?'

'No!' With a sense of humiliation she felt herself swaying dizzily on her feet. 'I don't want to listen to you any more. Can't you see how useless it is?' She pushed away from him, clinging to the last vestiges of her poise. 'Even if you convinced me to go back to you,' she said in a dry, brittle voice, 'how long would it last? Until the next race? It would be impossible, Philip. I couldn't stand that kind of ordeal.'

'You're very young,' he said quietly. 'Perhaps too young to have learned that the whole of life is taking risks. Nothing can be gained, nothing achieved, without taking risks. And the greater the prize, the greater the risk.'

'Not to my way of thinking!'

'As I said,' he repeated wryly, 'you're very young. Only being dead involves no risks, Lana. If you're looking for certainties in life, you're going to be a very disappointed woman. And love, of all things, involves the most risk of all.'

'Your kind of love, maybe,' she retorted fiercely. 'Not mine! I don't have to flirt with death in order to give my life a bit of spice! Or are you so jaded with the world's pleasures that you need the extra edge that two hundred miles an hour brings?'

'It's all a lot more practical than that,' Philip said flatly. 'Racing may seem like a playboy's whim to you. As a matter of fact, it scares the hell out of me. But it can bring my bank a fantastic amount of business. I calculate the risk involved against the potential for success. And the equation works out for me.'

'Not for me,' she snapped. 'You said yourself that some women couldn't stand it. Well, I'm one of them. I'm not as used to taking risks as you are. It's going to be bad enough from now on, every time I know you're out there, dicing with your life——' She looked up at him with dark, haunted eyes. 'Let me go now. *Please*. You've proved that you can hurt me——'

'But that's the last thing I want.' His fingers touched the smooth skin of her temple, brushing back the golden strand of hair. 'If you care as much as that,' he challenged gently, 'then how can you justify ending our relationship like this?'

'It's simply because I care that I'm doing exactly that,' she told him wearily. 'To spare myself the kind of hell I went through that day. And to spare you the ordeal of having a neurotic woman on your back the whole time.'

'I think I might be able to stand it,' he said with a wry smile. 'I'm afraid I'm not as logical as you seem to be, Lana. I can't simply order my heart to follow my head. Perhaps, as you say, it's because

I'm more used to taking risks. But I don't intend to let you go that easily.'

'The choice isn't yours!' She looked up at him with swimming eyes. 'I'm making the choice, Phil——'

His name ended in a gasp as he kissed her parted lips, sinking into their softness, tasting the tears on the bruised skin of her mouth.

She couldn't have resisted even if she'd wanted to; it was all she could do to lie in his arms with closed eyes, her fingers spread out against his heart, and let him kiss her. A kiss which made all words seem empty. A slow kiss that began with butterfly gentleness, until her lips softened and parted helplessly to allow him to explore the warm, wet secrets of her inner mouth. Dimly, she was aware of his heart pounding just under her palms.

The rigidity of her body dissolved against him, as though every inch of her skin wanted to cling to his, and she arched her throat to give him her mouth completely, surrendering unconditionally to the invasion of his kiss. His tongue was a torment, now thrusting and hard with passion in her mouth, now meltingly soft, and a voluptuous caress that seemed to set fire to her very heart.

Everything was melting in this flame, all her resentment against him, her cool arguments, the illusions she'd cherished about being impervious to him.

The truth was that she'd never been as close as this to anyone. Had never touched another human being's soul like this. Never known a man like this.

Another burst of laughter drifted to them on the breeze. What in heaven's name was she doing? The insanity of it made her panic, struggling weakly against him like a bird in a net. This was the very thing she'd determined not to let happen——

'For God's sake,' she gasped against his mouth. With the last of her strength she fought free of his arms, and sank against the trunk of the magnolia, covering her face with her hands to staunch the tears. 'Please go,' she choked. 'Haven't you done enough harm already?'

He was about to say something, but footsteps down the path silenced them both.

'Lana?' It was May Baragli, peering through the twilight. She giggled when she saw them by the magnolia. 'Oh! I—I thought you'd gone for a swim or something.'

'Lana was just showing me the garden,' Philip said in a toneless voice. 'Hullo, May. Nice to see you.'

'Nice to see *you*,' May said. She glanced uncertainly at Lana, who was standing in a bitter silence, hugging herself as though she were deadly cold all of a sudden. 'I didn't mean to—— I'm sorry if—if I disturbed anything.'

'You didn't,' he said heavily. 'I was on my way, in any case. I just dropped in for a few minutes.' He turned to Lana, his face impassive. 'Good night, Lana.'

'Good night,' she said in a choked voice. There was a turmoil inside her that was bringing her horribly close to tears again. She didn't watch as he walked up the path, out of her life.

May came up to her in concern.

'Oh, Lana, I could *kick* myself! I must have come barging in at the very worst possible moment!'

'You didn't.' She sighed shakily, feeling depression settle over her like a cloud. 'I don't know what would have happened if you hadn't arrived.'

'I did warn you,' May said gently, 'Philip Casson may be devastatingly easy to fall in love with, but there's a lot more to it than that.'

'He just doesn't seem to understand,' Lana said, sagging. 'I can't get through to him . . .'

'Yes, you can,' May nodded. 'But he lives in a different world. He's playing for big stakes. Massive stakes. You can't simply ask him to give it all up, no matter how much you care for each other. Philip isn't the sort of man to give ultimatums to.'

'What else can I do? You saw what he was like after the crash,' Lana said impatiently. 'You'd have thought he'd never want to get into another car in his life. But all he could think of was getting out there and winning again.' She struggled to find the words while May listened in silence. 'It's so—so stupid. So *pointless*.'

'Come on,' Lana sighed, 'I need a drink. And not an orange-juice this time.'

The party seemed hollow now, a collection of people posing and acting, their laughter and chatter meaningless. From beyond the tennis courts, where the cars were parked, she heard the soft growl of the Jaguar's engine. It faded towards the highway, and was gone.

He'd succeeded, she realised with a flash of bitter irony, in leaving her with the simple message he'd come to deliver. That no matter what she said, or did, or reasoned, she still needed him. Would always need him.

For a long time now she'd believed herself impervious to the kind of emotional passion Philip had just subjected her to. But she wasn't. There

was another woman inside her. A woman who
refused to obey the cold commands of her own
mind, who insisted on desiring, and loving, and
needing.

Philip had been right. She wanted him. Wanted
him as simply and as physically as any woman
ever wanted any man. Wanted him with all the
complex emotions of an adult woman's heart.

She'd thought herself over the worst. Philip had
kissed her, and now she was wounded all over
again, her nerves craving for him the way an
addict craves for a drug.

If her mind kept pulling one way and her body
in the opposite direction, it was going to end up
tearing her in half. Sooner or later.

CHAPTER EIGHT

LANA was hunched over the basin, washing her
hair on Sunday night when the telephone rang.
She was cursing silently into her towel as she
picked the receiver up.

'Yes?' she spluttered, dripping all over the hall.

'Hello Lana.' Her skin was suddenly hot all
over. There was no mistaking the deep voice. 'It's
Philip.'

'Oh,' she said, her throat too tight to say much
more.

'I'm calling about the contract. For your design
project. If you're still prepared to sign it, it's been
drawn up now.' His tone was even, businesslike,
holding no anger or irony. 'Do you want to sign?.

'To sign?' she said in a taut voice, wondering

whether he could hear her heart pounding, and
hoping religiously that he couldn't. 'Fine. Thank
you, Philip. Yes, I'll sign. I—when would suit
you?'

'Tomorrow afternoon, around three-thirty.'

'I'll be there,' she nodded, clutching the receiver
with a wet hand. 'Are you—are you all right,
Phil?'

'Fine,' he said easily. 'Still a bit bruised after the
crash, but nothing serious. See you tomorrow,
Lana.' The line clicked dead in her ear, leaving her
feeling suddenly drained.

She padded back to the bathroom. So, then.
Contact had been re-established. It remained,
however, to be seen what it would feel like trying
to conduct a business relationsip with Philip from
now on. Could she really stay as cool, calm and
collected in his presence as she expected him to be
in hers?

Judging by the way she felt right now, it wasn't
going to be easy.

She expected him to be hostile when they met
the next day, using that potentially oh-so-cruel
tongue on her. But as he welcomed her into the
penthouse suite that served as his office, he was
smiling slightly. Nor did he refer to the evening of
the cocktail-party.

'Come in,' he said, not touching her in any way.
'Bridgit will bring the contract through in a
minute, and you can read through it one last time
to make sure there's nothing you don't understand.' He looked magnificent. The pure wool suit
emphasised his lean, hard body, the dark silk tie
was fastened with a glittering diamond pin.
Powerful, almost brutally elegant, like a
Renaissance prince. 'How's your father?'

'He works too hard.' She managed a quick smile. 'But he's well, thank you.' Philip nodded, eyes cool as rockpools in the bronze of his face. She tore her eyes away, trying to stay expression-less. 'What happens after I sign the contract?' she asked.

'We find you a place to set up shop,' he replied, leaning back in his chair. 'Then we buy the equipment you need, and start hiring staff. After that, it's over to you to get things off the ground.' He tapped his pen on the blotter in front of him. 'The Bank's involvement will become progressively smaller—unless you run into difficulites, of course, in which case I'll step in. Otherwise, you'll be assuming full responsibility gradually, with the bank as a sort of guardian angel watching over you.'

'That sounds nice,' she said with another brief smile. It was hard, sitting here and talking to him like this. Much harder than she'd anticipated. The urge to touch him, run her hand over his arm, kiss him, was a sharp pang inside her. She dug her fingernails into her palm under the desk, knowing how easily those piercing eyes would be able to discover the truth of her inner turmoil!

The secretary came in with the two copies of the contracts, and laid them on the desk.

'Read it through,' Philip invited as the door closed behind her.

She sat in silence, paging through the brief forms. The terms were exactly as she'd already discussed them with Philip, the language clear and unambiguous. 'I'm ready to sign,' she said at last, looking up at him.

Philip passed her his heavy gold pen in silence. The moist, slick nib wrote black, with an air of finality. His name went beside hers, and then he blotted both copies.

'We're now formally pledged to each other,' he informed her with a wry smile.

It was a strange moment, bittersweet and slightly sad for her. She had no doubt that Philip's financial expertise would ensure the success of the enterprise she'd dreamed of for so long. But the feeling inside her was quiet warmth, rather than triumph. 'I'm glad,' she said softly.

'So am I.' He made a note in his pad. 'I'm going to send Bridgit home in five minutes. Feel like celebrating?'

'With what?' she asked cautiously.

'Nothing more wicked than Vienna coffee and something fattening,' he replied, eyes glinting. 'Come on. You look as though you need feeding.'

It was another rainy autumn day, and the wind tugged at their clothes like a beggar as they crossed the busy street. A few minutes later they were walking into the plush surroundings of Kafeeklatsch, an expensive little coffee-house that catered for Madison Avenue executives.

The Vienna coffee was delicious, and Philip watched with a half-smile as Lana disposed of a huge slice of rich Black Forest gateau, recovering her first bit of appetite for days.

'There,' he remarked, 'that's put a little more colour in your cheeks.'

'Did I look undernourished?' she asked, sucking the tips of her fingers and looking up at him.

'Somewhat.'

She was painfully aware of his gaze on her. 'Why are you looking at me like that?' she asked quietly.

'I was just thinking how strange you make me

feel,' he said, still smiling. 'Sometimes I feel that I'm escorting the most sophisticated and desirable woman in New York. And then sometimes, like right now, you make me feel like a father treating his schoolgirl daughter.'

'Oh,' she said blankly, wondering how to take that.

'It's your age,' he said wryly. 'You're still poised on the brink of womanhood. Sometimes you teeter back into adolescence, other times you seem about a hundred years old—emotionally, I mean.'

Lana buried her confusion by drinking off the last of her frothy coffee. If Philip only knew how very hard she found it to be close to him, yet to behave as though she didn't care—yet what he had said was so right. Since the accident, and the turbulent emotions it had unleashed in her, she was very conscious of her youth, of being only twenty-three, inexperienced and innocent in many ways.

Yet in others, she was becoming a woman with disturbing speed, with a woman's powerful emotions and needs.

'Let's go for a walk,' she said impulsively. As he glanced at his watch, she leaned forward imploringly. 'It's stopped raining—and it won't be for long.'

'Where?'

'Old Trinity Churchyard. It's only a little way from here.'

He smiled, crumpling his napkin. 'Trinity? A graveyard isn't exactly a cheerful place on a rainy day.'

'That's where I want to go,' she said. 'It's one of my favourite spots in the whole city.' The peaceful old churchyard was a green well of calm in the

mad commercial bustle of the south side, and
she'd spent several peaceful afternoons there in the
summer.

'Ten minutes, then,' Philip decided, and she
beamed at him.

They walked down the canyon of Wall Street,
and turned into the greenery of the Churchyard
opposite the Stock Exchange. As they strolled
under the dripping trees, the wet grass lush
underfoot, the incessant noise of the rush-hour
traffic faded behind them.

She led him to where the 18th Century Foxes lay
buried. The tombstones, some grey and almost
illegible with age, were scattered beneath a massive
chestnut tree.

'Some ancestors of mine,' she smiled up at
Philip. 'These are Foxes who emigrated to New
York in the 1700s.' Hands buried deep in the
pockets of her coat, Lana read him the
inscriptions, her green eyes reflecting the rainy
grey of the sky. She turned to him. 'Your
parents—are they still alive?'

'No,' he smiled gently. 'They're buried in an
English country churchyard, up in County
Durham. I never knew my mother—she died when
I was a baby, which meant I have no brothers or
sisters. Incidentally, it also made my father a
somewhat unlikely single-parent family.'

'I always see him as rather crusty and
formidable,' she ventured. 'He was a senior Army
man, wasn't he?'

'A career officer,' Philip nodded, looking
amused at her description. 'And he was both
crusty and formidable. Brilliant at his job, of
course, the sort of soldier who combined all the
traditional values with a thoroughly modern

outlook. But he had a soft centre that not many people knew about. I was very close to him.'

She assessed the absent expression in Philip's eyes, thinking of the way she missed her own mother. 'When did he die?' she asked softly.

'A few years ago. I was twenty-six, and well into my career at the head of L.C. It was very sudden. Heart disease—he pushed himself too hard, just like your father, just like all men of that type.'

'Like you?' she suggested.

'Not exactly,' he smiled. 'I've learned how to relax, something my father never understood. His death taught me how important it is to have things in your life apart from work and worry.'

'He must have been very proud of you,' she probed. 'After what you did with the Bank and everything.'

'I suppose he was proud of me in his way,' Philip said reflectively. 'He had a very strong sense of duty. He believed that one should do things in this life, achieve, succeed—so he'd always expected me to do well at something, it didn't really matter what.'

'He obviously passed his drive on to you,' she smiled.

'Yes,' Philip acknowledged the truth of her remark wryly. 'I'm afraid he did.'

'But didn't he expect you to follow him into the Army?'

'I think he'd have liked that.' The deep green eyes were still absent, miles away. 'But you can't always do what your parents want you to, can you? You have to follow your own star. After I left school, I had two excellent *entrées* to choose from—going into the Army like my father, or going into the Stock Exchange with my uncle.' He shrugged. 'The Army is a very cloistered world. You can go a long way, but strictly on rails. Deviate more than an inch either side of the path you have to tread, and that's it. Your career's in jeopardy. I couldn't see myself taking orders for the rest of my life, so I went into the Stock Exchange at eighteen.'

'Is that where you made the money to buy London Corporate?' she asked. 'On the Stock Exchange?'

'Yes.' His eyes glinted. 'I was a millionaire at twenty-three.'

'You're joking!' she gasped.

'I'm not,' he assured her with a grin. 'A paper millionaire, at least. But I was always looking for something more stable, something solid that would last. When the news broke that London Corporate was about to collapse, I saw an absolutely fabulous opening. I didn't have all that much experience of banking, but I had a good grasp of the whole financial scene—and I knew how to inspire confidence in sceptical people. The Bank of England was hesitating over coming to the rescue, but they weren't at all sure there was any future for L.C. I persuaded them that there was—and that I'd be the man to make sure of it.'

'I'll bet you did,' she said. 'You could persuade anyone to do anything you wanted, Philip.'

'Could I?' he asked ironically, meeting her eyes.

They walked on in silence. Her feelings about Philip caught her in the pit of her stomach. Gut reactions. Feelings of attraction, more powerful and basic than anything she'd known. Feelings of frustration so strong that they made her hands shake, her mouth dry. The way that husky voice of his could make her heart pound, the way he only had to look into her eyes to make electricity flicker along her nerves.

She looked into his eyes, and knew with utter certainty that he was reading her thoughts.

'This is nice, but I find it rather a strain,' he said quietly. 'Don't you?'

'Yes,' she whispered.

'I don't suppose it's possible you've changed your mind?' he asked in a husky voice.

The words made her ache, but she didn't answer, couldn't think of anything to say.

The rain started again, soft drops blurring the pale light, and Philip sighed. 'I'm sorry, stupid question.'

'It wasn't a stupid question,' she said miserably.

'It doesn't really matter, does it?' he said with weary finality. 'I have to meet some clients, Lana. I have to go now.'

'I see,' she said dully.

'We have to meet again quite soon. My staff have drawn up a list of likely premises for you, and we should start looking them over with a view to getting a lease.'

'Anytime, Philip.'

'Tuesday, then. I'll pick you up.'

Their farewell was almost formal, as though all the warmth between them had been washed away in the rain. He didn't touch her, didn't try to kiss her. As his tall figure was swallowed in the gathering dusk, Lana's eyes were blurring with tears.

Why did he always leave her with this pain inside, this mixture of wonderment and anger? She wiped the tears away roughly, and walked in the opposite direction, into the soft rain that was drenching Wall Street. Why was it always so damned painful?

She went to her father's for the week end again and although he ended up spending most of Saturday and Sunday sorting out a diplomatic wrangle involving some stateless persons, it was good to be around him.

She lazed in the garden with her notebooks and coloured pencils or relaxed with a pile of fashion magazines at the poolside, trying to get away from her problems.

On Monday morning she got back to her apartment with her head buzzing with ideas, and set to work on a series of six designs for silk which Bernat's had commissioned from her for their next stylebook, aimed at the vast homeknitting market.

Tuesday dawned cold, rainy and grey. The rain whipping at her windows when she awoke seemed to set the mood on the day for her, and the wind was a lonely sound.

Dressing up to go and look at a lot of empty old warehouses seemed a lot too much trouble. She pulled a tight sweater over her T-shirt and jeans, and got out the oilskin she'd sailed in while at College. There was almost defiance in the simple clothes, rather than the elaborate couture that would have been a more obvious choice. Philip had always seen her dressed to the nines. This, she thought drily, would be a change for him.

By contrast, Philip arrived in a beautifully-cut fawn coat which couldn't disguise the hard lines of his body, and a soft-brimmed fedora. His wolf's eyes drifted over her figure with merciless amusement, taking in the oilskin over her arm and the faded jeans that hugged her slim hips, then flicking up to study her tense face, framed with golden hair.

'You're not exactly an advertisement for your own fashions,' he purred.

'I'm not trying to be,' Lana snapped, feeling challenged, as always, by the raw male sexuality of his presence. Irrationally, she was now cursing herself for not having bothered to wear something more becoming. 'I thought I'd give you a change. Shall we go?'

'Why not?' he smiled easily.

The first two places he took her to were large, old-fashioned ex-shops on the fringe of the Bronx.

'Not nearly enough windows,' she commented with an air of finality about the second. 'This is even darker than the last place. You need light to make fine clothes, natural light. Besides,' she added, looking at the flaking walls and dingy ceilings with distaste, 'it isn't exactly upmarket, is it?'

'No,' he replied, unperturbed, 'but it's cheap. With a few coats of paint it could be made very pleasant.'

She shot him a sour look, and walked out.

The third place was more modern, and within sight of the skyscrapers of Manhattan.

'Is this any better?' he asked drily, watching her as she looked around.

'It's not bad,' she conceded, peering into the other rooms. 'Not as bad as the other places, anyway. But it's very small.'

'It also costs twice as much,' Philip said pointedly. 'The further upmarket you go, the more you pay for less.'

'Like everything in life,' she said, turning to face him with a smile.

He nodded. 'Yes, but the more you borrow from the Bank, Lana, the more you're going to have to pay back. You'll be on Fifth Avenue one day, but perhaps now's the time to be a little cautious.'

'I'd have thought that was the last quality you'd understand,' she shot back. He merely shrugged, as though to say he didn't care to bandy words with her. 'We'll bear this one in mind,' she decided. 'What's next?'

'Four hundred and twenty square feet on the thirteenth floor of the Eagle Star building,' Philip said, consulting the list. 'That's one of the big blocks on the South Side. And even more expensive than here.'

'That sounds more like it,' she said, showing her first hint of enthusiasm that morning. He led her wordlessly back to the Jaguar.

It had stopped raining by the time they got there, and the sky was patchily blue.

'Oh, Phil,' she couldn't help gasping as they let themselves into the empty offices, 'this is beautiful!' The floor was wall-to-wall carpeted, and the three wide rooms were given a delightfully airy feel by the huge windows that overlooked the bay. 'You can even see the Statue of Liberty!' She leaned on the window-sill, looking rapturously out. Her mood had lifted miraculously. '*This* is the sort of place I had in mind, right from the start.'

'Indeed.' Philip shut the door behind him, watching her with inscrutable eyes.

'You can see all the way to Ireland!' She turned. 'This could be a combination studio and office,' she decided, staring into the empty space with eyes that saw desks, drawing-boards, eager, dedicated people working busily at glowing fashions. 'The other two rooms could be making-up rooms, with all the machines and things. There's acres of space.' She pirouetted in the middle of the room, her arms thrown out, her face glowing with happiness. 'It's beautiful!'

Philip merely nodded, looking at her from under lowered brows. He walked through to the other rooms, glancing at the light fittings and power points. 'You like it?'

'I *love* it.' She paused, suddenly stricken with alarm. 'I can have it, can't I? I know it's going to be expensive, Phil, but it's so perfect. I'd be so happy here. Please say I can have it!'

'If it's what you really want,' he said with a hint of wry humour in his expression.

'It is!' Impulsively, she hugged him, their antagonism until now forgotten. 'It is!' He stiffened for a second as she hugged his lithe waist. Then his hands cupped her cheeks, tilting her face upwards.

'Mercenary little cat,' he growled, looking down at her through narrowed lashes. His eyes caressed the swell of her breasts under the close-fitting sweater, bringing a flush of colour to her cheeks. 'You have a very rare quality,' he said softly, 'of looking ravishingly sexy in almost anything.'

'How charming of you to say so,' she replied in a cool voice, her face staying flushed. It seemed to have been a long time since they'd touched like this, been this close.

He grinned wickedly. 'The word *sex* seems to bring the blood to your cheeks. Now, I wonder why?' He slid an arm intimately around her waist, pulling her close to his hard flank as they walked into the other rooms. He moved with a kind of instinctive animal grace that was quintessentially, disturbingly, male.

'I want you to be completely certain,' he said, glancing around. 'Is it big enough? Is it suitable?'

'It couldn't be bettered,' she said simply, clinging to his shoulder with both hands. 'It's twenty minutes to Fifth Avenue on the subway, it's glamorous, it's modern——' She shook her head. 'I don't want to see any more places, Phil. This is it.'

'Very well.' His eyes were still narrowed smokily. 'It's all yours.' It was as though an electric arc were sparking between them now, their mutual desire rising in response to the close contact. With a little gasp, Lana tried to pull away from him. His arms tightened like steel, drawing her back against him so that his hard thighs and stomach were pressed against her body.

'Let me go,' she said in a husky voice, her mind suddenly swimming.

'I want you,' he said, his eyes brooding into hers.

'You're taking advantage,' she protested, knowing he could feel the quivering in her body. 'We agreed——'

'We agreed nothing. You know how I feel about you.'

'And you know how *I* feel,' she said angrily. 'Stop this, Phil.' She was achingly conscious of his hard body against hers, half-terrified by his power over her emotions. God, he was so strong, so hard! No other man had ever felt like this, never. Her heart was beating wildly, and with a flash of self-disgust she recognised exultation in her own feelings. Exultation at being dominated by this tall man with the mouth that was at once both cruel and passionate.

'It feels so good to hold you again,' he growled, his hands drifting along the slender lines of her body. 'I've dreamed about you, Lana.'

'Stop,' she commanded, her eyelids closing heavily as she felt her will melting. 'I don't want this!'

'No?' His eyes mocked her with their disbelief. 'I do. I want you, every inch of you.' His voice became deep, velvety. 'Every silky, scented, exquisite inch.'

'Phil . . .' She clung to him, intoxicated by the caressing sexuality of his deep voice. His mouth was warm, taking hers with an authority she couldn't resist. As he kissed her, his tongue tracing the soft line of her lips, his hand caressed under her jersey, brushing across the smooth swell of her breasts, finding the delicate pearl buttons.

She moaned against his mouth as he eased her blouse open, touching her warm skin with his fingertips. Though his touch was feather-light, she shuddered uncontrollably, the blood rushing through her veins.

His tongue was probing her mouth, his hands discovering she was bra-less under the raw silk blouse. Lana's mind was beginning to reel; she was pure woman, responding with liquid, animal grace to the man she desired most in the world. Through half-closed eyes, she looked helplessly into the dark, male face above her, arching to him like a cat as he caressed the silky skin of her ribs, reaching the uptilted globes of her breasts.

'Philip, for God's sake,' she moaned, 'no . . .'

'You mean yes. You've longed for this as much as I have. Haven't you' He kissed her with a raw passion that shattered her emotions, his hand cupping her breast, brushing the aching peak of her nipple with his thumb.

Helpless, Lana let her arms twine around his neck, surrendering to the expert assault he was bringing to bear on her senses.

'Oh, darling,' she moaned, 'you're so cruel!'

'Is it cruel to need you?' he demanded fiercely. 'To need you, burn for you?'

'It's cruel when there's no hope for us, Phil!'

'Only because you say so,' he growled. 'As far as I'm concerned——' He kissed her hard. Her breasts were thrust against his hands, the pink tips stiff with the urgency of her desire, even though her body was recoiling from the intolerable intensity of the feeling.

He slid his hands down to her waist, pulling her against him so that she could feel the thrust of his desire, potent and passionate against her loins. 'We could make love right here,' he said, eyes stormy with need. 'Right here on the floor.'

With some ultimate remnant of self-control, Lana pulled herself away from him, dishevelled and scarlet-cheeked, gasping for breath.

'No,' she whispered, shaking her head. 'I won't let you, Philip. I made a decision, and I meant it——'

'God!' His whole being was taut with frustration and anger as he shook her. 'Who the hell are you to make decisions regarding the both of us?'

'My body is my own,' she said in a trembling voice. She couldn't meet those angry eyes. 'You still haven't realised that I'm serious about this, Phil. It's either your racing or me.' She turned away, pulling her crumpled clothes straight with numbed fingers. 'Tell me you'll give it up,' she said in a low voice. 'I need you as much as you need

me. Maybe more, because I——' She choked back
the words.

'You little——' He was with her in a stride,
crushing her in his arms, his kiss savage against
her yielding lips. Then he tore his mouth away
from hers, leaving her shaking in his arms. They
were breathing in unison now, fast and hard. 'You
drive me mad,' he said in a voice she barely
recognised. 'I could take you, here and now!'

'Is that the way you want me?' Lana whispered,
the golden hair tangled across her eyes. 'To force
me, like an animal?'

Philip's fingers bit into her arms like steel. Then
he released her with a whispered oath, turning
away from her. He walked to the window,
knuckles white as he gripped the sill and stared
blindly out across the bay.

'Damn you,' he whispered, his expression bleak.

Shaking with reaction and grief, Lana picked
her oilskin off the floor and looked at his broad
back timorously. 'I—I'm sorry,' she said in a small
voice. 'I didn't want this to happen. I—I'll find my
own way home.'

He didn't reply. Feeling broken, Lana pushed
through the door, and walked towards the
elevator, aching. Maybe it was best this way, she
thought painfully. Sometimes anger was the
cleanest emotion of all.

She went back home after the week-end and
worked feverishly on her preparations for the
autumn fashion show at the Lincoln Centre.

The Autumn Show wasn't *the* big New York
show of the year, but it came pretty close, and to
be chosen by the Committee as an exhibitor was a
fiercely contested honour among designers. Lana

had been thrilled by the invitation to contribute six outfits for the show, and had come up with what she herself recognised as exceptional designs—a Slavic-inspired range of swirling coats, dramatic boleros and full skirts, to be worn with capes and boots and lush fur hats. The colours, autumn russets and greys, were to be enriched with suede, fleece, embroidery and fur. It was, as one of the organisers had enthused, a fabulous range.

Getting the outfits ready, working with the tailors and knitters and seamstresses to produce the clothes just right, took up all her time and energy; by Wednesday night, the colours and lines seemed to dance like demons in front of her eyes, and her concentration was all shot to hell. She left the work unfinished, and went to bed early, even though restlessness was burning her up.

In her dream, Philip was beside her. His skin was warm under her touch, his body taut and hard. Her lips parted under his kiss, her reactions at once timid and passionate. She felt his caress all the length of her body. His fingertips brought ecstasy, brushing her breasts, their hard peaks, the flat plane of her stomach.

She heard her own voice call to him, commanding him to love her, and was trembling when he came to her. His face above her was dark, his eyes green slits. Their lovemaking was slow, infinitely gentle until the end, when his arms crushed her to him, his kisses fierce on her eyelids, her throat, her mouth. She felt her hips arch to the devastating thrust, her legs clasping Philip's lean, muscular waist. His body was fiery inside hers, filling her deeper and deeper, as though he wanted to plunge into her womb itself.

Realisation came with a profound shock. They

were husband and wife. This wasn't just pleasure, not just sex. It was life itself. They were making a baby. That was what they wanted, to make her blossom, bring forth fruit.

And then there was flame.

An evil crimson flower of flame that exploded all around them, engulfing them, choking their lungs with thick, oily black smoke, stripping the skin from their bodies. Philip's face became a skull, horribly grinning . . .

Lana awoke in a lather of sweat, gasping for air, trying to shake off panic. She went on trembling legs to the window and flung it wide on to the warm night.

'Oh God,' she whispered unevenly. The memory was still so real. The textures of his body were still burned into her skin, sweet in her mouth. The hard muscles of those broad shoulders; the thickness of his hair, its smell, all mingled with the horror of that accident . . .

Her bedroom was stiflingly hot. She pulled off the T-shirt she slept in, and padded into her studio in her briefs, on the verge of tears. What the hell was happening to her? In the cool moonlight, she leaned against the wall and gazed at the tools of her trade—the big draughtsman's drawing-board, the tables of paints and crayons, the sewing-machine standing silent in a corner, the piles of catalogues and magazines, the ghostly shapes of the models she used, their impossibly elegant poses strangely life-like in the pale light.

She'd never been like this, so uncertain and afraid. She'd never let a man affect her in this way. Men had been fair game to her, people stupid enough to do you a favour because they lusted after your body. Now that had all turned against her, all that shallow rubbish smashed and thrown up into her face.

Through the wide window the lights of New York spread in a vast web into the night. A city that never slept. He was out there somewhere, the man who'd left her wounded.

So much for being cool.

CHAPTER NINE

SITTING in the audience with her father on the great night, bathed in the glitz and glamour of the occasion, it was all worth it.

There was a style about this occasion that was like nothing else in the business; the designs didn't have the daring, frivolous quality of the spring parades. These were classical designs, sobered by the prospect of snow and icy weather. Her own designs followed a beautiful selection of knitwear from Calvin Klein, which had the audience gasping in admiration.

Lana's Slavic designs, however, got a more robust response.

'Listen to them clap,' Wetherby Fox said, almost in awe, as the tall models pirouetted and strutted across the light-saturated catwalk. 'They love you, Lana!'

Excitement bubbled over in tears as she listened to the roar of approval echoing round the great auditorium. She could hardly see the models; she simply clung to her father's arm, overcome with the moment. Lightbulbs were exploding all along the catwalk as the fashion photographers snatched their shots. The pictures, Lana knew, would be in tomorrow's papers, in the Sundays by the week-end, and in the glossy magazines by next week. New York, as ever, was setting the pace for the whole fashion scene.

And she was part of it.

The party afterwards was vast and noisy. 'I still can't quite believe it,' her father called, passing her a glass of champagne over the heads of an excited gaggle of reporters. 'You're famous, Lana!'

'Hardly,' she smiled, still slightly emotional. 'But it's a good start.'

'I thought they'd never stop clapping.' He ushered her through the throng to a quieter corner of the room. It was slow going; hundreds of strangers seemed to know her name, and wanted to congratulate her. 'This is one occasion,' he observed, as they found a vacated chaise, 'when more people seem to know you than me!'

'You don't mind?' she asked, smiling at the lined, aristocratic face she loved so well.

'Of course not. It's wonderful to see your career taking off like this.' He toasted her affectionately. 'You look absolutely magnificent, too.' He leaned forward. 'You know, I've got a confession to make.'

'Confess away,' she invited, sipping the fizzing champagne.

'When you started that design course in Chicago, I thought it was all just a hobby for you.' He sought for the words. 'A pastime. Something you'd amuse yourself with until you got married.'

'Oh, yeah?' She looked at him with sparkling green eyes, ravishingly pretty on this spectacular occasion.

'I didn't have the slightest idea it would turn out

like this for you.' He waved at the noisy throng all around them. 'Did you?'

'Yes,' she said, still smiling. 'I did, Dad.'

'And where is it going to end?' he asked gently.

'You mean—am I going to settle down and marry some nice young man, and forget all about my career?' she supplied.

'I wouldn't have put it in such crude terms.'

'That's the diplomat in you,' she laughed. 'The answer is that I don't know,' she went on, more seriously. 'I love my work, and there's a long way for me to go. But there's also a vacant space in my life. I wouldn't like to spend the rest of my days in the fashion industry. It's just that I haven't met anyone I could be serious about yet.'

'Not even Philip Casson?' he asked with those damnably sharp eyes on hers.

She couldn't help her cheeks from flaming. 'Philip isn't even in the running, Dad,' she said sharply. 'He's a long way out of my league—out of my generation, even.'

'I see,' he nodded, apparently accepting her reaction. 'And the others—like Lionel Webber?'

She pulled a wry face. 'To be honest, Dad, I can't see myself marrying any of the men I know. They're so limited, so childish. They just never seem to grow up.'

'Hmmm,' he said thoughtfully. 'That depends who you're measuring them against.' She dropped her eyes, wondering just how much he'd guessed of what had happened between her and Philip. 'You'll have to accept that you're a lot more mature than most people are at your age. But I wouldn't give up hope,' he smiled. 'Especially not if someone's in the habit of giving you gold.'

'Gold?'

'That pendant you're wearing,' he pointed out mildly. 'It's new, isn't it?'

'Oh, this,' she said, even more flustered. It had been weeks since she'd worn the piece of eight pendant; but tonight, for some reason, she'd wanted to feel its heavy, cool presence against her breast-bone. 'Phil gave me this coin, so I had it set. Do you like it?'

'It's beautiful,' he said, lifting it to study it. 'A Spanish *piastre* if I'm not mistaken. Philip must care a great deal for you, Lana.'

'Oh, I'm sure he doesn't,' she stammered, reddening. 'In fact I know he doesn't—he's just an acquaintance, really.'

'And not even of your generation,' he agreed smoothly, eyes twinkling.

'That's right!'

'Do you ever think about England?' he asked unexpectedly.

'England,' she mused. 'Of course I think about it. But we've been in America so long that it almost feels like home to me now.'

'Yes.' His expression changed. 'I suppose that tonight's as good a time as any to tell you, Lana. I'm going to retire in a year's time.'

'A year?' she blinked in surprise. 'But Dad! You're only fifty-two.'

'I'm nearly fifty-four,' he said. 'And I'm entitled to retire at fifty-five if I want to. I'm going to take it, Lana. I'm tired, girl. I need a break.'

'A break, yes,' she urged. 'But you're at the peak of your career——'

'Which is an excellent place to stop,' he smiled. 'There are too many other things I want to do. Hybridise roses, breed spaniels, just listen to the grass grow. Since your mother died,' he went on in a quieter voice, 'a lot of the pleasure has gone out of my work. I find I'm just going through the motions. And it's a lot lonelier and harder without Marjorie.'

'Oh, Dad,' she said, putting her hand on his. He covered it with his own.

'When you left home to work in New York, I fooled myself that you'd be back some day. But tonight, watching all this——' He shook his head. 'You're making your own life now. It's only right that you should. And some day soon you'll meet the right man, and want to settle down. Its the right time for me to leave diplomacy and go back to Shropshire. I've been gallivanting around the world for too long now. I need some peace and quiet.'

She sat in silence for a few moments, looking at him. 'Oh, Dad,' she said at last. 'I've been so blind.'

'No, you haven't. You've just been young.' He patted her cheek. 'You're growing up so fast, though. You've got so much going for you. All this for a start.' He looked around the glittering hall. 'And after Philip sets up the business for you, you'll be completely fulfilled.'

'It's not the most important thing in my life,' she said with a small smile.

'It was the last time I asked,' he laughed. 'But I meant fulfilled in a creative sense. I wouldn't presume to judge your love-life.' He smiled, then hesitated. 'I'd be a lot happier if I thought you'd be spending at least some of your time in England.'

'Of course I will!' she exclaimed. 'As much time as I can. I'm going to be marketing my clothes in London as well as New York, Dad.'

'Good,' he smiled. 'I can't pretend that I viewed the prospect of our living in different continents with equanimity. I love you, and I want to be as near to you as possible. I'm not fool enough to believe we could live in each other's pockets, and the very last thing I want is to stand in the way of your personal development. But you're all I've got now.'

'You'll always have me, Dad,' she said quietly.

The intimacy of their moment was suddenly ruptured by a blaze of flashguns. The press photographers had coincided with the arrival of a television camera team with one of the models in tow, still wearing one of Lana's designs.

A strangely familiar woman's face was smiling at her.

'Lana Fox? I'm Joanna Shapiro, NBC News Team. Could we have an interview? I won't keep you long.'

'Go where glory waits you,' her father murmured with a grin. She squeezed his hand, and got up to face the white-hot lights.

It was midnight before she got away. She hugged her father good night, and watched as the Consulate limousine drove him away, then went down to the basement to pick up her own Porsche.

The streets of Manhattan were quiet at this hour. The night air was cold and damp, and ghosts of steam were writhing at the iron grates of manholes. She drove down East 79th Street, feeling melancholy wash over her. At the corner of First Avenue, she stopped, and looked up at the glass-and-steel tower where Philip Casson had his apartment.

A longing to see him, stronger than any logic,

pulled without warning at her heart. It wasn't so much want as need. Just to see him, hear his voice.

She wrestled with herself, eyes closed, fists clenched on the wheel. Yet the hunger inside her was too strong to argue against. He drew her, like a moth to a candle, and she could not fight against the brightness of his flame.

She drove up in front of the Maling Building, locked the car, and walked into the lobby of the apartment block, her heart thumping.

He took so long to answer her nervous knock that she was beginning to think he was out, or had gone to bed. Then the door opened. Standing tall above her in the doorway he smiled gently.

'A midnight visitor. I thought you'd be around sooner or later.'

He wasn't remotely surprised to see her. Her knees were shaky, but she kept her face expressionless, not wanting him to know how much courage it had taken to come up to his apartment.

'Can I come in?' she asked huskily.

One eyebrow arched mockingly. 'Of course.'

Her heart was in her mouth as he let her in. Philip was casually dressed in faded denims that hugged his hips and a sleeveless black T-shirt. His naked arms were sinewy with muscle, the casual clothes making him strangely sexy in this ultra-formal setting. The veneer of culture he'd worn at their last meeting was gone; he was now somehow animal, dangerous.

She couldn't help flinching as he lifted her coat off her shoulders.

'Am I disturbing you?' she asked nervously.

'I was just sorting through some boring paperwork.' He gestured at the heap of papers on the coffee-table. They looked at each other for a second. The formality of her white gown contrasted sharply with his casual denims and cottons. 'Need a drink?' There was a panther's grace in his walk as he moved to the group of decanters. She hadn't missed that 'need', and had to smile wryly.

'I suppose I do.'

He gestured her to sit down, and she sank into the crisp comfort of an armchair. 'Scotch or bourbon?'

'Either,' she shrugged. 'I'm not a drinker.'

'Scotch, then. I've never really got used to bourbon.' He passed her a chunky crystal tumbler with a pool of amber at its heart. God, he was handsome! She couldn't look into those eyes, could hardly trust her voice not to shake.

'Now,' he said softly, 'what game shall we play?'

'I came here to talk,' she said quietly. 'Not to play games, or to flirt, or to fight you. Just to talk.'

'That's not a bad idea.' He raised his glass to her. 'You look delightful, as usual. Sorry I'm not dressed to receive you.'

'You look fine.' She dropped her eyes from the bronzed, naked column of his throat, where the crisp hairs curled. His denims were wickedly tight, clinging revealingly to the power of his thighs and loins. She gulped at her whisky.

'So.' He smiled. 'What have you been doing with yourself?'

'This and that.' She felt ridiculously small under that grey-green scrutiny. 'Trying to stay away from you, mostly.'

He threw back his head, his throat rippling with laughter. 'That's honest, at least.' She smiled wanly, and he nodded. 'I like to see you smile.

Your mouth was made for smiling.' His eyes glinted. 'What access of courage has brought you here, Lana? I thought I was supposed to be the big bad wolf.'

'You must be very insensitive,' she replied, 'if you can't understand my feelings, Philip.'

'I must be very insensitive,' he agreed with irony. 'And you have the monopoly on sensitivity, don't you?'

'I didn't say that.'

'You implied it.' He studied the whisky against the light. 'I like your father. He's a good man. But he just didn't have the time to raise a spirited daughter, after your mother died. You've been allowed to get away with murder ever since you were a child.'

Lana watched him through narrowed eyes. 'I never saw you as one of those men who believed women should be silent, demure and obedient.'

'I'm not,' he smiled. 'But you're very wilful.'

'Because I won't give in, and do exactly what you want?' she challenged. 'You're a dictator, Philip. To dictators, anyone with a mind of their own is wilful!'

'Wilful people,' he corrected smoothly, 'are people who are too stubborn to do even what's right and good for them!'

'A category into which you fit very neatly,' she said waspishly. 'So—that's the way you see me? Stubborn and wilful?'

He cradled the tumbler in competent hands, his eyes never leaving her face. 'Partly. You're a very gifted designer, of course, which gives you a right to be wilful, I suppose. Otherwise I wouldn't be taking any financial chances with you. You're also a very alluring person. Not just in a physical

sense,' he said with a wolf's smile. 'There's a
vulnerable quality to you that is very appealing.
You haven't had it as easy as might seem. You've
been travelling round the world ever since you
were born. A lot of people might dismiss you as a
rich bitch, but there's a deep insecurity under that
glossy façade. You need love and reassurance
more than most people.' He drained his glass. 'As
a matter of fact, that's a rather endearing side to
your nature.'

'Really,' she commented with a vinegary smile.

'You've always exploited your looks, getting
what you wanted because you were beautiful. You
tell yourself that you're being clever, that you
don't need love.'

'Maybe I don't,' she shrugged defiantly, trying
to hide her deep unease, and wishing she'd kept on
driving tonight.

'Except that you're frigid. Oh,' he smiled drily at
her outraged expression, 'I don't mean frigid in the
sexual sense. I know too much about you to
suggest that. You're emotionally frigid. It all
comes down to the question of taking risks. You
won't take any.'

'I won't stand by and watch you kill yourself, if
that's what you mean!' Lana's eyes blazed at him
like angry emeralds.

'There,' he sighed. 'I've upset you.'

'Please don't worry about me.' Why was she so
absurdly vulnerable to the things he said to her? It
had been a crazy blunder coming in here, to have
jeopardised the fragile calm she'd built up over the
past days. She must have been mad. 'If you don't
mind,' she said stiffly, getting to her feet, 'I think I'd
better go, Philip. I don't want to go through all this
again. I'm sorry to have interrupted your evening.'

'Don't go.' He was standing in her way, reaching for her shoulders to stop her. 'I've said I'm sorry.' His eyes were deep, compelling. 'The last thing I want is to hurt you, Lana.' He drew her close enough for the tips of her breasts to brush his chest. Then he pulled her to him with a tenderness she couldn't believe was possible.

'You're so young,' he said softly, his breath warm in the silk of her hair. 'You don't understand how deep feelings can go, how much they can hurt . . .'

'Oh, I do,' she whispered. Giddy with the closeness of him, she wondered why he couldn't hear her heart pounding so loudly within the circle of his arms. The pain inside her was like a lump of ice, aching to melt in his warmth. 'You'd be surprised at how much I've learned in the past few weeks, Philip.'

His lips caressed hers, intoxicating as hot wine, and she closed her eyes, every thought draining from her mind as she parted her lips for his kiss.

It was long, slow, infinitely sweet. The warmth that melted her from within spread down into her belly, into her abdomen, settling like molten honey in her loins. She could feel him against her, his body hard and so much bigger than hers, yet moulded to her so closely that they might have been made for one another's embrace.

Her fingers were trembling as she touched his hair, caressed his cheek, lost in the wonder of him. She strained against him, longing with amoral innocence to be free of their clothes, their skins touching . . .

They sank on to the sofa, Philip hauling his top off impatiently.

'My love,' he whispered hungrily. 'Thank God you came tonight. I've been so desolate without you.'

'And I've ached for you,' she shuddered. 'My love, my man ...' She crooned over his body, her hair tumbled over her face to give her some shy modesty. He was magnificently male. There was so little spare flesh on his body that the marvellous tracery of his muscles was outlined under the bronzed velvet of his skin.

'Are a man's nipples sensitive, like a woman's?' she asked, almost naïvely, touching them with her fingertips.

Philip's arched eyebrow mocked her. 'I have no idea. Why not see?'

Lana leaned forward touching the hard tips with her tongue. He tasted faintly salty, erotic. As she kissed him he shuddered, gasping deep in his throat and thrilling her to her core.

'No more,' he commanded, but his husky voice was shaking. She kissed the velvety skin of his chest, the pulsing muscles of his stomach, revelling in the taste and the smell of him. *'Stop,'* he said fiercely. Exalted in her love, she wanted him to want her as much as she wanted him, wanted him to be helpless, at her mercy; but he was far too strong, pushing her back and dragging the gown off her almost roughly.

She was almost naked as he laid her back, his mouth hungry, marauding, tracing the lines of desire across her fine skin. Under her hands the muscles of his back were tight and hard.

She wanted to be right for him; not prim Lana Fox, repressed and arrogant—but a true, responsive woman.

'I don't know what to do,' she said in a strained voice, her eyes closed. 'I'm so afraid, Philip!'

'Let me teach you.' It was as though he wanted to kiss every inch of her skin, taking a blazing delight in her body, in the planes of her stomach, the swell of her breasts, her mouth, the scented hollow of her throat; then down to the curve of her hip-bone, tracing the smooth line of her thigh with his lips. 'I want to love you the way I've never loved a woman before,' he whispered. 'I wanted you the second I saw you, Lana. Each time we've met since, I've wanted you . . .'

His breath was warm against her abdomen, his fingers sliding the silk briefs away from the mystery of her surrendering thighs, his lips kissing her smooth skin shamelessly, worshipping her.

It transfigured her, this adoration of her body by such a powerful, dominant man; as though he were making her more than a woman, making her the centre of the world. Her body arched like a bow in response, feeling as though her heart would burst inside her.

'Love me,' she pleaded. 'Love me . . .' And never mind about afterwards and what she would feel in the morning. Philip was hers, here and now, and nothing else mattered.

The burr of a telephone slid into the silence.

He held her for a long moment, then gently released her. She felt weakness wash over her as he lifted the ivory instrument off a coffee-table. She was ready for him, ready to be made love to, here and now.

'Philip Casson.' He paused, then sighed, sliding back against the cushions with the 'phone in his lap. 'I won't be a second,' he told Lana, covering the mouthpiece with his hand. 'Hi, Roger. Welcome back to New York. How's the car? Is she ready for the circuit tests?' Something in the changing note of his voice told her that his attention was shifting entirely to the subject of his damned racing-car. She tried to clear the clouds of passion from her mind, feeling sudden disgust at her own desire, so hot and thoughtless. She clenched her teeth tightly, beginning to ache all over again. Of all the sickening anticlimaxes! It was almost as though she was deliberately being taught a painful lesson.

'That sounds marvellous,' he was purring, his eyes flicking to Lana. 'I'm glad you've managed to squeeze an extra few horsepower out of her. That'll give us an edge over the Lancias. What about maximum speed? Any idea?'

'Damn you!' Lana hissed. Close to tears, she walked across the room on shaky legs, pulling her gown closed. What madness was possessing her? She stared blindly out at the million lights of New York, wondering where in God's name she was going to. The emotional toll of the evening was beginning to show in her ragged nerves. It was bad enough to be betrayed by her own body, to have thrown all her resolutions to the winds; it was too much to have to listen to Philip planning his next race with Roger Preece!

'I'm sorry, Roger,' he was saying, his voice sounding genuinely regretful, 'but I can't test-drive her this week. No, there's no question of that, either. As it happens, I have to leave New York the day after tomorrow.'

Lana spun from the window to stare at him in alarm. Leave New York?

'Yes, I'm afraid so. I'm booked on the eleven-thirty flight to Japan. I have a big meeting with Tanaka on Monday morning. They want me to finance a range of factories in England. Big business for the bank, and potentially very good for the ailing economy. But I'm going to be back by the twenty-sixth. If you can get the car and the trailer down to Indianapolis, we could meet there over that weekend, and start getting the car into shape. That should give us enough time to prepare for the qualifying circuits.'

Lana felt a chill touch her at his mention of the famous racing-circuit. Indianapolis. The race was due in a very short while; by now all the teams would be in full swing.

Philip smiled at something Roger said. 'Yes,' he said with a husky laugh, 'I'm going to win, Roger. You can bet your damned boots on that!'

'Good news?' Lana asked in a vitriolic voice as he replaced the receiver.

'The new car's ready—and she's faster and more powerful than ever.' He shrugged. There was a glint in his eyes still. 'Don't look so outraged. I'm going to win this race, Lana. And the next, and the next.'

She turned away from him, hugging herself in that characteristic gesture of pain. 'When will you be back from Japan?' she asked in a quiet voice.

'A matter of a week. Will you miss me?'

'Why should I?' The forced carelessness rang false, even in her own ears. What a fool she was being, what a blind, damned fool. It seemed with everything she said or did she made herself look more ridiculous in front of Philip, delivered herself more surely into his spell.

She felt his touch on her shoulder.

'Why did you really come here tonight?' he asked quietly.

'I was passing the tower on my way home,' she told him, feeling as though that had been days ago. 'On my way back from the autumn fashion show.'

'Ah. I'd forgotten about the autumn show.'

She turned to face him with a wry smile. 'You don't really give a curse about women's fashions, do you?'

'You're a client,' he shrugged, then softened it. 'I do care about what you do, Lana.' She hung her head, afraid that he'd see her pleasure in his words shining in her eyes. He tilted her chin up to look into her face. 'Was it a success?'

'Pretty good,' she said awkwardly. 'They seemed to like the designs, anyway. I had several offers to buy afterwards.' His close scrutiny made her feel weak all over again, her body aching for his touch, and she turned away from him, knowing she must leave, now or never. She picked up her coat. 'I'm sorry I disturbed you, Phil. I'd better get back now.'

'Stay if you want to.'

She slipped her arms into the sleeves, and looked at him wryly. 'Not a chance.'

'I thought not,' he said drily. 'You've turned back into your prim and proper little self at the mention of racing.'

'When—when is Indianapolis?'

'The twenty-ninth,' he replied, meeting her eyes. 'Want to come?'

The twenty-ninth. It was a horribly short time away. She felt exhaustion wash over her, and turned to go. 'I'll be thinking of you, Philip. Please take care.'

'I always do,' he said with a grim smile. 'Be thinking of me, won't you?'

CHAPTER TEN

NEWSPAPER reports about the fashion show were exceptionally good over the next few days. One or two reviewers had found her designs a little too avant-garde, but everyone had mentioned them, and most had raved. One of the biggest papers printed several photographs, describing her as one of the most exciting young designers in New York. She cut the reports out, and pasted them in a scrap-book.

The telephone calls went on all day, and sometimes into the evenings. Many were from shops or companies asking for designs, sketches, anything. Significantly, there were half-a-dozen from various fashion houses, sounding her out about ready-made garments. She put these on file.

On Thursday, she hurried out to Susanna Nardi to answer an urgent call Erica Gilbert had put in that morning.

'We want more,' Erica told her flatly, once the preliminaries were over. 'Anything you can supply. Can't put it plainer than that.' The thin face, with its pencilled eyebrows, disappeared behind a plume of Turkish smoke for a moment. 'You're becoming a sensation, Lana,' she proclaimed like some oracle from the cloud. 'Susanna wants this shop to be associated with that sensation. After all, we saw your talent early, didn't we? I mentioned your intentions of launching Fox Enterprises to her. She's distinctly interested in a contract—when you get things settled, of course.'

'That's fine,' Lana nodded.

'You seem to be taking the whole thing very casually,' Erica remarked.

'I'm just a little tired, I guess.' Lana brushed the hair back from her face. 'Don't think I'm not very flattered by Miss Nardi's interest.'

True, she hadn't had much sleep since Philip had left New York. But depression, more than anything, accounted for her dispirited air, depression about the race. Indianapolis was haunting her. Philip's need to do well in his new, more powerful car was going to be urging him on to greater speeds, greater risks. And she was beginning to regret the fact that the tangled relationship between them might be adding to the distractions on that powerful mind.

'You shouldn't work too hard,' Erica said sympathetically. 'You're doing very well as it is, Lana.'

'Thank you.'

'If you don't mind me saying so, you look as though you're a little run down. It's an easy thing to forget about holidays when you're self-employed. Why not take a little break somewhere for a week or so?'

'I wish I could, but I've got——' She broke off, not knowing what to say.

'Are you having man trouble?' Erica's jackdaw eyes had picked out the heavy gold pendant at her throat. 'If you'll excuse the question?'

'Something like that,' Lana sighed, certainly not wanting to discuss it with Erica Gilbert. *Man trouble*. The phrase seemed so very inadequate. Erica's sharp brown eyes narrowed.

'You're not pregnant?' she enquired.

'God, no.' Lana smiled wanly.

'It's just that you seem to keep going into a kind

of trance. Anyway, it's up to you.' Her sympathy exhausted, Erica turned back to the notes on her cluttered desk. 'We don't want to put any restrictions on what you produce, Lana. That's up to you. As a hint, though, we generally do well with occasional clothes. Evening gowns, suits, things people buy for a wedding or a première. We'd like you to just let your imagination run wild, and see what you come up with. In a way, the more extravagant, the better. What we're interested in are the things that please *you*. Interested?'

'I'll do what I can,' Lana nodded.

'Obviously, the fee is negotiable,' Erica said smoothly, clearly taking Lana's unenthusiastic expression as a criticism of Nardi's last payment. 'You think of a figure, and let us know. Okay?'

'Okay,' Lana nodded. Having a miserable expression, she reflected wryly, seemed to be an excellent sales-technique. Erica had been giving her the red-carpet treatment this morning, something not all designers received in the Fifth Avenue shop.

'I'll start work on some dresses as soon as I can, Erica,' she promised, standing up. 'I have some ideas which came up while I was working on the fashion show, and which I haven't used yet. I'll take another look at them and see what develops from there.'

'Attagirl.' Erica's eyes glittered as she pulled the butt of her cigarette from the little ebony holder and ground the spark out. 'That's the stuff. That show was a triumph for you, you know.'

'You're very kind to say so,' Lana said sadly, thinking of what had happened afterwards, 'but I'm afraid it was rather a qualified success . . .'

She was depressed, leaving the shop. She was

missing Philip so much, her mind plagued by doubts and fears that wouldn't let her rest. Had she really made the right decision about the only man she'd probably ever love like this?

May had been right. Confronting Philip with an ultimatum hadn't been sensible. It had only placed intolerable strains on both of them; looking back, their relationship had been a string of disasters. Yes, she'd acted sensibly—according to her lights. But she'd also caused them both a great deal of suffering . . .

She hadn't sickened him of her, not yet; but sooner or later he was going to grow sick of trying to change her mind, and would lose his patience with the chase. It was beneath a man like Philip to go chasing an elusive virgin around the town. And after all, hadn't he promised to consider giving up racing once this season was over?

Yes, but promises like that were easily broken. And there were still six more races this season, an intolerable burden of fear and anxiety for any human being to put up with. In the final analysis, any choice she made was the wrong one.

In the final analysis, all she had to cling to was her own courage.

The weekend loomed ahead, bleak and frightening. On Saturday, at Indianapolis, the qualifying laps would be taking place, each driver pushing his car to the limits of its speed to ensure a good place on the starting-grid. And on Sunday, the race itself, six hours of snarling chaos, watched by countless millions across America and the world.

On the way back from Nardi, Lana was weighing up the prospect of sitting at home over the weekend, trying to work, and trying not to switch on the television set. Depression washed

over her. Or there was an alternative; Lionel
Webber was always keen for her to partner him at
tennis. Unlikeable as the country club set were,
they would at least provide a distraction for her on
Saturday.

And then, on Sunday, she could go to her
father's, and spend the day with him. She got back
to her apartment, and went straight to the
telephone.

'Webber Oil? I'd like to speak to Lionel Webber
Junior please . . .'

'Did you hear the television?' Lionel asked,
glancing at Lana slyly as they drove out of the
country club car-park. 'Your Philip got himself
pole position for the race tomorrow.'

'I heard,' Lana said quietly. The television had
been on in the lounge, as usual, and the coverage
of the qualifying circuits had coincided with their
salad lunch.

Philip had been fastest round the track. There
had been an accident, too. During the practice, a
well-known German driver had smashed his car
into the barriers, and was now in intensive care. It
had seemed a horrible omen.

'Pity about poor old von Kurig,' Lionel went on
casually. 'Seems he's got internal injuries. Broken
ribs punctured his spleen or liver, or whatever.'
Lana turned away, sickened, and Lionel grinned as
he noted her reaction. 'Is that why you played
such rotten tennis today? Worrying about your
lover-boy?'

'Philip's not my lover-boy,' she said tightly.

'Oh, come,' Lionel snorted, 'you're as trans-
parent as a sheet of glass, Lana. I saw your face
this afternoon. And your lack of concentration

lost us that second game, too.'

'I'm sorry if it was my fault,' she snapped, upset by Lionel's heavy-handed mockery. 'Yes, I *am* worried about Philip, if you really want to know.'

'He's a good driver,' Lionel shrugged. 'So am I, as it happens. Easily as good as your Philip. Care for a demonstration?'

'Not right now,' she said shortly. 'And not on a public highway. You're not exactly in Philip's class, Lionel.'

'Oh no?' As though wanting to impress her, he accelerated the Porsche hard, the needle flickering up to the eighty mark.

The tyres protested faintly as he swept the car round a tight corner. Lana was slightly breathless as she said, 'Come on, slow down, will you?'

'I know what I'm doing,' he grinned. 'You worry too much, honey.' He changed back into fifth gear, and trod hard on the accelerator. The growling motor responded with a surge of speed that had Lana's stomach turning inside her. She was wishing now, as she sometimes did, that the Webber family weren't quite so damned pushy.

'I can't help worrying, Lionel. It's my car.'

'Sure you don't want to sell it?' he offered. Lana muttered something rude and he laughed, swinging the wheel. She had to cling to her seat as the Porsche took the corner at the old oak tree much too fast. She was frightened, and a little angry, too—not least with herself for not having been more tactful about his driving prowess. If a patrol car happened to be lurking in one of these leafy lay-bys, there'd probably be enough beer on his breath to add a drink-drive charge to speeding.

The New Jersey landscape sped past, bright in the evening sunlight. 'Sit back and enjoy it,' he grinned, sparing her a quick glance. His face was slightly flushed. 'I'll show you how this baby *ought* to be driven!'

'Please,' Lana urged awkwardly. She wasn't used to pleading with anyone. 'Slow down, Lionel.' She winced as the tyres squealed round another corner. The road was deserted, but if they were to meet someone coming the other way on one of these sweeping bends——

'What a motor.' He changed back into fifth gear, and Lana braced herself against the seat as he had to brake fiercely for a sharp turn. *'Lionel.'*

'Okay, okay.' He slowed down a few miles an hour to around eighty, and looked across at Lana with a smile. 'I thought you enjoyed great driving.'

She didn't answer, merely folded her arms sullenly and stared out of the window. Lionel suddenly looked into the rear-view mirror.

'Jeez,' he said under his breath. He pulled aside slightly as a red Mustang blasted past them on the outside. 'Holy smoke.' The other car's tail lights glowed for a second at the next bend, and then it had swept out of sight.

She glanced at Lionel with some amusement. It wasn't often anyone overtook Lionel J. Webber Jnr. He looked blank for a second, then, with a savage grin, accelerated hard to catch up.

'Oh, come on,' she said impatiently, 'let it go, Lionel.'

'Not a chance.'

'Lionel, I forbid you to race that man in my car!' She might as well not have spoken. They were just in time to see the red haunches of the other car disappear round the next bend.

'It's a Mustang,' he said with satisfaction. 'We've got a good ten miles an hour on him!'

'There are speed limits,' she reminded him sharply. 'And this is my car!'

'Don't be such a droopy-drawers.' He took the corner with more speed than finesse, and they skidded perilously wide. They were slowly catching up with the Mustang now. The other driver, a man a few years younger than Lionel, gave them a brief glance over his shoulder, then said something that made his companion, a platinum blonde, laugh.

Lana clung to the strap as Lionel rocketed in pursuit, the greenery blurring around them.

'For God's sake,' she muttered, knowing it was useless to argue now. To someone with Lionel's tiny mind, being overtaken by the Mustang was some kind of insult to his manhood, and he had to recoup his honour. The next series of bends had her swaying from side to side, helpless in the gravitational forces generated by the car.

The Mustang was no closer as they came out on to the straight. It seemed to flick through the bends as though it were on invisible rails. The younger man, Lana realised gloomily, was a lot better driver than Lionel.

'He's fast,' Lionel said grudgingly. Two or three saloon cars whipped past on the other side of the road, and then Lionel was forcing the Porsche towards the Mustang, his jaw clenched. The speedo needle was on 120, and the howl of the engine just behind them rose to an ear-piercing pitch. 'Slow *down*,' she begged, shouting against the noise. Lionel wasn't listening. He pulled out to overtake, exultation bright in his eyes. The red car accelerated smoothly away, sweeping into the next bend with a mocking snarl of exhausts.

Lionel swore savagely. The bend was almost too much for him, and Lana felt genuine terror as he wrestled to keep control of the car. For a horrible second they were skidding, and then they were out of it, swaying from side to side as they hurtled under a bridge and on to the straight. Ahead of them, the Mustang had already overtaken a truck, and Lionel had to brake hard before swinging out and overtaking in his turn. Lana got a glimpse of the trucker's contemptuous expression. She could read what he was thinking. Rich kids, burning up the roads at everyone else's risk and expense.

'He's playing with you,' Lana said tightly as she saw the blonde's teeth flash in a derisive grin through the windscreen.

'I'm going to get that bastard,' Lionel gritted. Lana sat in rigid silence as he pursued the other car towards the setting sun. What a stupid way to die, trying to soothe Lionel Webber's infantile vanity.

Again, he hurled the Porsche up towards the Mustang, and pulled out viciously in an attempt to overtake.

'Lionel!' Lana screamed. The red car coming straight towards them was swerving wildly. White-faced, Lionel stamped on the brake. The Porsche snaked across the road like a switchback, just missing the rear of the Mustang. Lana saw the road blur as they crashed through the high grass at the edge of the road, and bounced spine-joltingly back on to the pavement. The other car flew by with a furiously blaring horn.

Lana was pressing her knuckles against her mouth, trying not to scream again. Lionel accelerated back after the Mustang, but his eyes had a glazed look, and she knew with dreadful certainty that they were going to come unstuck.

The next bend was too tight, and in mid-corner, he jumped off the throttle awkwardly.

The ice-blue car whipped round like a stone from a slingshot. She felt her head thump into the pillar as the Porsche chased its tail in a complete spin. The scream of the tyres was like some huge thing in pain.

The bank was rushing at them, the world tilting madly. And then, frozen in her mind like a photograph just before the crash, the air was full of shattered glass.

Hospital noises. Hospital smells.

Lana drifted between consciousness and waking, her body numb, her mouth dry. There had been pain, a lot of it, but that was over now. Now she had to rest.

The gentle dark was calling her, offering her a refuge where she could hide away from the pain. In case it came back.

But there were voices, outside in the corridor. Voices that were trying to keep low, despite the anger that was vibrating in them.

'You can't talk to me like that!'

'Keep your damned voice down. Does it ever occur to rich kids like you that a car can be a lethal weapon?' Lana turned her head weakly on the pillow, knowing that voice instantly as Philip's.

'We were only having a bit of fun.' The other voice was Lionel Webber's, sounding petulant, angry and frightened. 'Things just got out of hand, that's all.'

'Out of hand?' Philip's voice was like a lash. 'If Lana dies, Webber, God help you. Because I'll see you stay behind bars for the rest of your life.'

But I'm not going to die, Lana thought,

struggling against the dream-world that was enveloping her. I'm alive, my darling, and I need you so much. With a supreme effort, she forced her eyes open. Through the glass partition, she could see Philip. He was wearing faded denims that hugged his lean hips, and a used-looking black leather jacket over a polo-neck sweater. The dark shadow of beard gave him a fierce, tired look. A wave of longing for him made her eyes swim, but she was too numbed to call to him.

'Don't threaten me, buddy.' Lionel appeared uninjured apart from a puffy bruise on one cheek. Thank God, then, he'd got off a lot more lightly than she herself had. 'We've got the best lawyers in New York!'

'You're going to need them,' Philip rasped. 'The driver of that Mustang was here this morning. He told me about the way you were driving. He wants to make a statement to the police.'

'You don't seem to know who I am,' Lionel blustered.

'Oh, I do,' Philip said silkily. 'I know your father well. You must be even stupider than he is.'

'Watch your tone, buddy!'

'As for your idea of fun,' Philip said in a voice that cut like a razor's edge, 'I intend to see to it that you don't drive another car for at least two years. You're a dangerous cretin.'

'Listen, Casson,' Lionel said thickly, stepping forward, 'you talk pretty big——'

'Yes?' Philip was easily as big as Lionel but dark and lethal, infinitely more dangerous. A black Miura bull, she thought suddenly, ready to slash and kill with wickedly sharp horns. Frightened for Lionel's sake, she opened her dry lips.

The tiny movement caught Philip's eye. He

pushed swiftly through the door, and was at her side, the colour draining from his face.

'Lana,' he said in a voice that shook slightly. 'Can you hear me?'

All she could do was nod. Happiness spilled over into a tear that slid down her cheek. For the first time she realised that her head had been bandaged. The smoky green eyes that were staring so intently into hers widened with relief.

'Thank God. Don't try and say anything.' He kissed her lips with infinite gentleness. Hers were so dry that they felt almost papery against his. He touched her cheek with his fingertips, looking down at her with so much love that she had to close her own eyes against the tears. 'You've been unconscious for nearly two days,' he said quietly. 'Do you remember the accident?'

She nodded slightly again. Lionel was standing silent and sullen in the doorway.

'You had a nasty concussion,' Philip went on. 'Stitches to your head, stitches to your arms and leg. They might hurt a bit, but it's all right now. D'you understand me?'

She forced her lips to move, forced them to form his name. 'Phil . . .'

'I love you,' he said quietly, kissing her eyelids, which had begun to ache now. 'And I'm never going to let you go again. Now I have to tell the doctors you've come to. All right?'

She moved a bandaged hand in slow-motion panic, trying to stop him from going.

'I'll be back,' he said, his deep voice certain. 'I'll be back before you know it.'

She watched him stand up and usher Lionel out of the room, unmistakable male grace in every line of his body.

The light was fading again, but this time she didn't try and fight it. She had something to take with her now, a wonderful something to cling to in the gentle darkness.

The next time she surfaced out of deep sleep, the curtains had been drawn, and late afternoon sunlight was washing the room. She felt better, clearer-headed, but more aware of the tight pain of stitches and bruises all over her body. She was also more conscious of being very weak.

Considering the speed the Porsche had been going, it was a miracle either of them were alive at all.

She turned her head slowly on the pillow. Philip was in an armchair in the corner of the room.

'Phil,' she whispered. But he was asleep with his dark head resting on his outflung arm.

Instinctively she knew he'd been with her all the time. There was a sweet irony in her having awoken just when her patient watcher had fallen into weary sleep.

She lay still, content to just watch him, her heart full of the deep, life-giving love she had for him.

The strangest thoughts were drifting through her mind. He was so tall, so authoritative; he stood out from other men, making them all seem somehow inadequate. *What are we to him?* May had asked. *Little girls, that's what.* She'd been so afraid of that adult, mature quality in him, the force of character that had made him such a commanding figure in his field. It awed her. It gave him an obstinacy that had sometimes made her almost hate him.

In another sense, it was what made her love him. It made her long to shed her own puppyish immaturity, and reach him. Earn his respect, his love.

Now, more than ever, she knew that she couldn't live without Philip Casson any longer. She wanted it all. A future together. Marriage. Philip's children in her womb . . .

Could it happen, even now? His presence here said

maybe. But she'd led herself up a blind alley, and the

only way out was back the way she'd come. An abject apology. Maybe that was the only way.

Calling on every nerve in her body, Lana hauled herself upright in the hospital bed. She was shaky, her bandaged arms aching.

Philip stirred as the small sounds disturbed his sleep. He opened dark-rimmed eyes at her, looking as though he thought it might be a dream. Then he jerked into full wakefulness.

'You're supposed to be lying still,' he scolded gently, helping her to sit up against the pillows. 'How long have you been awake?'

'Just a few minutes.' Her voice wasn't much more than a whisper. He kissed her so lightly that she had to smile. 'I'm not made of glass, Phil. For God's sake, hold me!'

It was wonderful to feel his arms around her, to feel his warmth against her body.

'Oh, my love,' he whispered. 'I thought I'd lost you.'

'You won't shake me off that easily,' she said with eyes closed in bliss as she rested her head on his shoulder. 'God, I feel weak! Have you been sitting there all day?'

'I've been sitting there since Saturday night.' He touched her cheek, looking into her eyes. 'Today's Monday, Lana. You've been in hospital for three days now.'

That took a while to sink in. She was so muzzy.
She'd lost so much time! 'Dad?' she questioned
instinctively. 'Is he——?'

'He was here earlier in the afternoon. He'll be
back soon. And when he sees those beautiful
green eyes open, he's going to be a very happy
man!'

'Is he upset?'

Philip's dark eyebrows lifted ironically. 'Now
what do *you* think?'

'I'm sorry,' she said shakily, thinking of the
agony he must have been going through as she lay
in unconsciousness. She clung to his hand with
both of hers. 'Didn't mean to worry everyone.'

'It wasn't your fault, you poor darling.' He
rubbed her hand with a cheek rough with stubble.
'It was your boyfriend Lionel Webber.'

'I heard you telling him off,' she remembered,
tracing the passionate line of his mouth with her
fingertips. She remembered the lethal anger in his
face and voice. Anger that had translated as love
for her! 'Don't be too hard on him, Phil. He's just
a kid.'

'He's a——' he didn't finish the sentence,
kissing her palm instead. Lana looked into his
face, finding the sunlight in his eyes.

'I've been lying here thinking how much I love
you,' she said, holding his eyes. 'Thinking how
much I need you, Philip. I don't ever want to live
without you. I don't care about anything any
more—life's too short for anything but love. And I
want all of mine to give to you.'

'Life is too short.' He bent to kiss her again, the
musky hint of passion lurking on his lips this time.
'Do I need to tell you that I love you, Lana? You
must have known it for months now.'

'I—I've prayed,' she said. 'Damn these tears. I want to tell you so much——'

'There's all the time in the world for that.' He kissed her salty mouth tenderly, lovingly. 'There'll be no more barriers between us, my love. For now, you need rest. You'll be in this place for at least the next few days, until all your stitches come out.'

She lay back against the pillows, still weepy with happiness.

'Did you win your race at Indianapolis?' she asked, smiling.

Philip laughed huskily. 'You can't have heard me. I've been right here since Saturday night. Indianapolis went right ahead without me. I've been too busy following your little performance.'

She stared at him blankly. 'You've missed your race?'

'I tried to call you on Saturday evening, after the qualifying laps. You weren't at your apartment, and when I 'phoned your father's house, his secretary told me you'd been——' His mouth tightened. 'Been in a smash.'

'Oh Phil!'

'I got hold of one of the marshals, and withdrew from the race immediately. I was on a plane to New York by eight.' He smiled at her stricken expression, his unshaven chin and untidy hair somehow making him all the more attractive. 'Until you opened those bewitching eyes, no one could be really sure you hadn't sustained brain damage to some degree. So I waited.'

'Oh Philip! I'm so very sorry about your race——'

'You won't be when you hear what I've got to say.' His smile faded. 'It's all over, Lana. I've told

Roger Preece to find a new driver for the Jag. My racing days are done, for ever.'

'I don't believe it,' she gasped.

'It happens to be true. I'm only sorry that it took a near-tragedy to get the message through my thick skull.' He rose, and walked to the window, his face bathed in the golden light as he looked out. 'It shames me to admit how cruel and selfish I've been, Lana. I'm asking you to believe me when I say that I never knew. I never really knew what you went through until I found myself in the same position. Sitting beside you all those hours, wondering whether you were ever going to wake up——' He broke off, turning to her with a grim expression. 'It was a slice of hell, Lana. The same hell you went through, that day at the clinic. The gut-wrenching fear that takes you when you're wondering whether the only person you'll ever love is going to live or die. The way your future suddenly stretches ahead of you, empty and sterile.'

'Phil,' she whispered, stretching her arms out to him. 'Come to me.'

He sat beside her, holding her hands and smiling at her wryly. 'I'd convinced myself that you were being a neurotic fool, you know. I was so sure, so pig-headedly confident that I knew best, that I had to go ahead and win those races.' He shook his head. 'I was scared half to death by it, you know. All drivers are. But I'd psyched myself up to doing it, and I was damned if I'd let you take my martyrdom away from me. I would have been damned if you'd died in that crash. There would have been nothing left of me.'

'I'm so sorry you had to go through all that, Philip.' She looked at him with blurred eyes. It was a miracle. A painful one, but a miracle nonetheless, that had brought them together at last!

'We've been given another chance. That's all that matters, Lana. God isn't as good as this to everyone. You and I must be a chance in a million.'

'Another chance,' she repeated, nodding as she thought how close they'd been to disaster so many times. 'Our only chance. I'm going to take it with both hands, my love.'

'So am I.' They smiled into each other's eyes, and she knew they'd found the perfect understanding that had eluded them for so long. 'Thank God you've understood at last, Phil. You know you could have had me on any terms—but to risk your life like that——'

'Hush.' His lips stilled hers. 'It's all over now. The end of an era, I swear it. Married men have responsibilities, you know.'

'Is that—is that a proposal?' she asked in a husky voice.

'It's more like an order,' he said. But the uneven note in his voice pleaded for her confirmation, and she laughed softly.

'The answer's yes, to either. Always yes!'

The door opened silently, and a nurse glanced in with bright eyes.

'Sorry to disturb you,' she smiled. 'But Sir Wetherby Fox is here to see Lana.'

'Oh, Dad,' she said as her father came uncertainly into the room, looking as though he couldn't quite believe she was real. 'Dad, are you all right?'

'You're awake,' he said, his hands trembling as he caressed her hair. For once those piercing eyes were blurred. 'This is wonderful news!'

'She seems to be recovering her old self with remarkable speed,' Philip smiled. 'I think the worst is over now.'

'Thank God for that,' the Consul-General sighed, laying his hand on Philip's shoulder. 'Philip's been at your bedside for days, Lana. Did you know that?'

'Yes. And there's something even more wonderful,' she said tremulously, 'that you have to know.'

'I think I can guess what it is,' her father said gently. 'Philip's a gentleman, Lana. He asked my permission before consulting you on the subject.' His solemn expression broke into a delighted grin. 'Do I have to tell you what my reaction was?'

Lana cradled the brandy-glass in her hands and stared out of the window at the silver ribbon of the Thames and the treescape of Richmond beyond. The house was a Palladian-style villa on the bank of the river, its exquisite, curved front overlooking a delightful informal garden that merged into reed-beds beyond an old boat-house. It was one of the most romantic places she'd ever seen, the atmosphere of culture and peace within its walls like nothing she'd experienced before. Sharing this place with Philip was going to bring her a deep, lasting pleasure.

Philip had decided that they'd needed a week's break from New York—and the media interest that had surrounded the announcement of their engagement.

'Besides,' he'd smiled, 'I'm selfish enough to want you all to myself, even before we marry. And you need some tranquillity, some beauty, to help you forget the accident.'

Compared to the brash pace of New York,

London had seemed impossibly dignified and ancient, its muted greys softened by the years. The smell on the streets was achingly familiar, bringing Lana waves of nostalgia as they'd enjoyed the city hand-in-hand, like a pair of children. And then, later, he'd taken her up in his private helicopter, soaring high above the city in an unforgettable aerial tour. She hadn't been in the Learjet yet— that was a thrill yet in store!

It was a kind of pre-honeymoon, a time of discovery. Discovery which had sometimes been almost too exquisite to bear. A familiar, warm feeling uncurled in her stomach as she remembered the nights they'd shared, the love they'd made . . .

She'd been awed by the Bank. It was easy to see why aristocratic and moneyed people liked banking here; in addition to Philip Casson's genius, they got all this—the kind of class and style that she'd come to believe was extinct in England. The Georgian front was timelessly graceful, the patina of time having polished it like some precious thing. Yet the interior had hummed with the smooth efficiency of a well-maintained computer!

She touched her temple. The fine scar was hidden in her hair already. Today they'd been sailing on the Thames, and she'd been able to haul on the sheets with as much energy as she'd always had. It was almost a pity that her excuse for being pampered was slipping surely away!

She loved to curl up in this window-seat, watching the swans on the smooth current of the river. They were due back in New York by the end of the week, but it seemed so very distant right now. She was here with Philip, in his world, and nothing else seemed to matter. The contentment that only love can bring had sealed her spirit, ironing the kinks out of her mind.

'Tired?' he asked, coming to sit beside her at the window.

'Yes—but very, very happy,' she said, gazing up at the dark, handsome face she'd come to love so well.

'You're so beautiful.' Philip took her hand in his, tracing the line of her palm with his fingers. 'You take my breath away sometimes.'

'I bet you say that to all the girls,' she said, nestling into his arms. 'Are you really going to be happy with just me for the rest of your life?'

'Oh, I should think so,' he said gravely.

She laughed softly. 'I'll work very hard to make it happen, my love. But I can't have been easy to love when you first met me.'

'It was uphill work occasionally,' he admitted. 'The first time I saw you, you bowled me over. But you also used to infuriate me, with your arrogance—and that very special brand of self-sufficiency.'

'I was little more than a child you know,' she defended herself. 'I only turned twenty-three a week ago, remember?' She tilted her head to let him see the bright diamond earrings that glittered among her golden hair. They matched the stone that blazed on the third finger of her left hand. Gifts from Philip, generous and beautiful as the man himself.

'Your loveliness fascinates me,' he smiled, 'child or not. And the closer I looked, the more there was to you. I found courage and humour, a woman's heart that drew me like a magnet, irresistibly. Loving you came as naturally to me as breathing.'

'And to me. When I first saw you, at the pool,'

she told him quietly, 'I'd never seen a more beautiful man in my life before.'

'And I spent most of that afternoon,' he grinned, 'deciding exactly how I was going to make love to you.'

Lana's cheeks coloured. She pursed her mouth in a self-mocking *moue*. 'And there I was imagining you really thought I had talent!'

'Oh, your talent is very real,' he said seriously. 'You're brilliant, my darling. Maybe as brilliant at your job as I am at mine.'

'La, what modesty,' she teased, adoring him.

'Financing a Lana Fox fashion house happens to be an excellent proposition,' he smiled, 'and we're going to do it, together. You're going to be up there with the top fashion houses of the world one day.' He touched the soft swell of her breast with a possessive hand, making her shiver. 'How lucky I am,' he said quietly, 'to be marrying not only a desirable, adorable woman, but a brilliantly talented designer into the bargain. I used to spend hours walking round American Fashions and Nardi, and all the other shops who carried your clothes, just looking at them and thinking of you. I've fallen in love with your designs too, Lana. They're beautiful. They have the grace, the imagination, that only the very best art has. We're going to have such a wonderful, fruitful life together, my darling.'

She looked at him with eyes that were suddenly serious. 'If you knew how much I need you—never leave me again, never.'

'I never intend to.' He held her close, kissing her yielding mouth with fierce passion. 'Not even if you order me to, the way you did after I crashed that Jag.'

'I was horrible,' she said, clinging to him.

'You were trying to save my life. But it was rather like a bomb going off,' he smiled reminiscently. 'I was quite in awe of you.'

'But not enough in awe of me to stop racing,' she teased.

'That took an even more painful lesson,' he said ruefully. 'But I couldn't stay away from you, no matter what you said or did. There's a wonderful, magic quality about you, my love. I can't describe it—vulnerable, *alive*, deeply feminine—which always fascinated me. I came to need it the way a plant needs light. You gave me light, a light I'd never known.'

'You're my whole life, Philip. I'd have nothing without you. Be nothing.'

'That's what love is,' he said tenderly, stroking the glossy sheen of her hair. 'I went through misery in those first weeks of our separation. I resented what you were doing, almost hated you. I felt terrible. I hungered for you, but you wouldn't let me touch you—and there was nothing I could do about it, nothing I could do to make you listen to me.'

'But didn't you know how much you obsessed me?' she laughed shakily. 'I dreamed of you, Phil. My whole body was crying out for you.'

'As mine was for you. Somehow I simply couldn't stay away from you.' His mouth was warm, commanding, his kiss like spiced wine flooding her veins, intoxicating her instantly. She ran her fingers through the crisp curls of his dark hair, her lips opening like a flower under the fierce heat of Philip's desire. She clung to him for long ages, drinking in his kiss, taking him into her heart and her mind for ever. There was wonder in her misty green eyes as they at last parted. 'I've done nothing to deserve you, Phil,' she said in a trembling voice. 'I can hardly believe that it's true.'

'It's been true for a long, long time,' he said quietly. 'The more I saw you, the deeper my feelings grew. It was a desperate need to possess you, to keep you close to me. In the end I was forced to recognise it for what it was—love. By then, our relationship was a hopeless tangle, and I could see that despite your response to me, you were more or less permanently angry with me. That made me frustrated and angry in my turn, unable to control my feelings, yet unable to back down and admit how callous and selfish I was being in keeping on racing. Can you find it in your heart to forgive me?'

'If you can forgive me for being such a shallow, vain little fool,' she said, touching his lips with wondering fingertips. 'If I was ever bitter towards you, it was only because I was so afraid for you . . .'

He rose, tall and dominant, and pulled her to her feet. 'Come,' he commanded huskily.

'Where to?' she blinked, rising on unsteady legs.

'The master bedroom.' As she hesitated, he scooped her up in his arms as though she'd been thistledown, and grinned wickedly down at her. 'I want to show you my etchings.'

'You're a rose,' he whispered, his lips caressing the satiny peaks of her breasts. 'As perfect and as lovely and as fragrant as a rose.' She cradled her head in her arms, too full for words. The evening had brought a glorious sunset, the crimson light bathing their naked bodies through the wide window.

'Is it always going to be like this?' she asked dreamily.

'Always,' he smiled tenderly. 'Always desiring, never being sated with each other. That's what love is. An infinite variety of combinations of desire.'

He leaned on one elbow, tracing the sweet lines of her body with his fingers, until the need for him leaped through her veins like a golden river.

'You make me ache for you,' she whispered, arching to his touch. 'This will always be the perfect time and place for me, Phil. In bed together, naked.'

'And for me. Always.' He reached out for the champagne-bottle, and poured the last glittering splash into the glass they'd been sharing.

'Don't tell me you're running short,' she teased, accepting the glass from his hands.

'I have a cellarful of the stuff,' he assured her, his eyes glinting.

'Good.' Lana held the glass up to the light, the sunset flooding the wine with ruby, and smiled at him. 'In which case I'll polish this off myself.' She poured the champagne into her mouth.

'Piglet,' he murmured, coming to her in mock-anger. His lips found hers, demanding a share of the golden wine. She parted her lips, letting the champagne run into his mouth, cool and fragrant. Their kiss deepened into passion, the love between them flaring up and igniting like a furnace. He slid on to her, his hard body tense and eager, pulling her fiercely against him. Her soul opened to him as it had done in her dream. Only this time it was real, real and perfect and wonderful in a way that no dream could ever be. She was Philip's—going to be his wife for ever, united so completely that no one and nothing could ever part them again.

'There's so much to talk about,' she whispered, her palms caressing the powerful muscles of his back.

'Afterwards,' he growled.

'But all we do afterwards is make love again,' she said, laughing softly, blissfully.

'There must be limits,' he said, smiling down at her. 'When we reach them, we'll discuss things— like the wedding.'

'You could have a Princess if you wanted,' she sighed. 'Are you quite sure you only want me——?'

'I can see I'll have to prove it,' Philip said huskily. 'Again and again.'

'Yes,' she whispered, her mouth opening under his kiss. 'And again . . .'

Harlequin Presents

Coming Next Month

887 LOVE ME NOT Lindsay Armstrong
A schoolteacher prepares to lead on an Australian boat designer. That's what he did to her sister, after all! But she doesn't count on his infinite charm—and her sister's deceit!

888 THE WINTER HEART Lillian Cheatham
After taking the blame for her sister's tragic carelessness, an artist escapes to Colorado to work as a secretary—never dreaming that her new boss chose her specifically.

889 A VERY PRIVATE LOVE Melinda Cross
While covering an Egyptian Arabian horse show in Kentucky, a reporter traveling incognito uncovers a reclusive American entrepreneur, also in disguise. He's the man she's been waiting for—to make or break her future.

890 THE OVER-MOUNTAIN MAN Emma Goldrick
A motorist stranded in the Great Smoky Mountains seeks refuge at the home of an inventor who imagines she's in cahoots with his aunt to end his bachelor days. What a notion,…

891 THE MAN IN ROOM 12 Claudia Jameson
What with the blizzard and the flu epidemic at her mother's Welsh country inn, the man in room twelve is too much. And for the first time in her life, Dawn loses control of her emotions.

892 DARKNESS INTO LIGHT Carole Mortimer
The security-conscious new owner of the Sutherland estate warns his gardener against falling in love with him. But the only danger she can see is that he might break her heart….

893 FOREVER Lynn Turner
Can a surly ex-army colonel and a bogus nun find love and lasting happiness? Perhaps, with the help of a guardian angel to get them through the jungle alive!

894 A MOMENT IN TIME Yvonne Whittal
The shock of seeing each other again shatters the composure of a divorced couple. For her, at least, love lasted longer than a moment in time, though she isn't so sure of him.

Available in June wherever paperback books are sold, or through Harlequin Reader Service.

In the U.S.
901 Fuhrmann Blvd.
P.O. Box 1397
Buffalo, N.Y. 14240-1397

In Canada
P.O. Box 2800, Postal Station A
5170 Yonge Street
Willowdale, Ontario M2N 6J3

WORLDWIDE LIBRARY IS YOUR TICKET TO ROMANCE, ADVENTURE AND EXCITEMENT

Experience it all in these big, bold Bestsellers— Yours exclusively from WORLDWIDE LIBRARY WHILE QUANTITIES LAST

To receive these Bestsellers, complete the order form, detach and send together with your check or money order (include 75¢ postage and handling), payable to WORLDWIDE LIBRARY, to:

In the U.S.
WORLDWIDE LIBRARY
901 Fuhrmann Blvd.
Buffalo, N.Y. 14269

In Canada
WORLDWIDE LIBRARY
P.O. Box 2800, 5170 Yonge Street
Postal Station A, Willowdale, Ontario
M2N 6J3

Quant.	Title	Price
_____	**WILD CONCERTO**, Anne Mather	$2.95
_____	**A VIOLATION**, Charlotte Lamb	$3.50
_____	**SECRETS**, Sheila Holland	$3.50
_____	**SWEET MEMORIES**, LaVyrle Spencer	$3.50
_____	**FLORA**, Anne Weale	$3.50
_____	**SUMMER'S AWAKENING**, Anne Weale	$3.50
_____	**FINGER PRINTS**, Barbara Delinsky	$3.50
_____	**DREAMWEAVER**, Felicia Gallant/Rebecca Flanders	$3.50
_____	**EYE OF THE STORM**, Maura Seger	$3.50
_____	**HIDDEN IN THE FLAME**, Anne Mather	$3.50
_____	**ECHO OF THUNDER**, Maura Seger	$3.95
_____	**DREAM OF DARKNESS**, Jocelyn Haley	$3.95

	YOUR ORDER TOTAL	$_____
	New York and Arizona residents add appropriate sales tax	$_____
	Postage and Handling	$___.75___
	I enclose	$_____

NAME _____

ADDRESS _____ APT.# _____

CITY _____

STATE/PROV. _____ ZIP/POSTAL CODE _____
WW-1-3

Can you keep a secret?

You can keep this one plus 4 free novels

HARLEQUIN BRINGS YOU

Janet Dailey

★ **AMERICANA** ★ ★ ★

A romantic tour of America with Janet Dailey!

★

Beginning in June, enjoy this collection of your favorite previously published Janet Dailey titles, presented state by state.